Night to Dawn 47

Marge Simon: pages 12, 28, and 79

Chris Friend: pages 16, 27, 49, 78, and 88

Sandy DeLuca: front cover and pages 6, 43, 50, 61, and 82

Elizabeth Hattie Pierce-Collins: pages 23, 72, 74, and 84

April Lafleur: pages 17 and 68

Denny E. Marshall: back cover and pages 10, 33, and 81

Lonnie D. Weems: page 20

Vincent Davis: pages 3 and 60

Night to Dawn No. 47, April, 2025; Copyright 2025 by Barbara Custer. All rights revert to individual author and artist after publication. ISSN # 1542-1430; ISBN: 978-1-937769-86-4

Night to Dawn is a semi-annual publication of fiction, poetry, artwork, articles, and review.

Orders, editorial, and queries: Barbara Custer, P. O. Box 643, Abington, PA 19001

Email: barbaracuster@hotmail.com or ntdsubmissions@gmail.com

PayPal orders: venus1021@juno.com.

Submissions: ntdsubmissions@gmail.com; Web: www.bloodredshadow.com

Pickings and Tidbits

Top of the balloon to you! ☺

The year 2024 was a bear, and I know several people who would agree with me. I'm glad it's over; I hope for a pleasant 2025. Old Man Winter was temperamental, as he usually is. Most times, I wanted to hibernate. However, I got a nice yield on tomatoes last summer and continued having fun with pumpkin recipes and refreshments. I'm looking forward to planting season, with an eye toward tomatoes and peppers.

Night to Dawn 47 favors vampire fiction but with a unique twist. Ditto for the other monsters. For starters, Lee Clark Zumpe gave a unique twist to the zombie with "Wake of the White Death," and his brand of zombies is as deadly as traditional ones, if not more. "A Message Sent to the Patient Heavens" made me stop and think. Can humans work well together? It didn't appear so on the moon, but they could have had a good thing. Aliens are watching over us to see if we can learn from our mistakes. One day, they might visit. Speaking of humans, I found the human monster more frightening in Linda Barrett's "Journey" than the aliens. By far. Christopher T. Dabrowski's shorts often revolve around war involving human monsters. On a romantic note, "Gone," a haunting prose of love and heartbreak by Sandy DeLuca, held me spellbound, wondering if the protagonist would reunite with her old love.

The real-life Bathory was as bloodthirsty as the one in Matthew Wilson's "Lady of the Castle." The records are unclear as to how many people she killed. She mostly stuck to servants but then murdered a noblewoman. That crime got her tried and sentenced to life imprisonment in her castle. The queen on the front cover could have been Bathory.

I can truly relate to the premise and humor in Rod Marsden's "Do Not Touch My Computer." Like the protag, I need my sleep and computer time. Woe betides the villain who gets in the way of my computer and mattress!

The vampire in Hillary Lyon's "Chasing the Ragged Flag" loves to keep, shall we say, mementos of his victims. Curiosity killed Fred as he demanded the vision reveal itself in Marc Shapiro's "Back Up." Remember the funhouse at the carnival you enjoyed as a kid? The scariest moments have nothing on Marge Simon's "Carnival of Ghosts;" there's no escaping this funhouse. Hal Kempka's back with "Date Night," warning us not to get any car with strangers or at least get to know them over lunch before we do. I could picture vampire Carrie saying: "I don't drink … coffee."

I was pleased to receive an illustration by Lonnie D. Weems, and hope to feature him in future issues. Sandy DeLuca did the front cover, interior illustrations, and short story. Denny E. Marshall did the back cover, interior illustrations, and poetry. Marge Simon contributed poetry, prose, and interior illustrations, while April Lafleur illustrated two of the stories. Elizabeth Hattie Pierce continues to bring her incredible illustrations, and along with his own illustrations, Chris Friend contributed some poetry. Vincent Davis is back with more of his comic strip illustrations, and he'll appear in the NTD pages for the foreseeable future. I did have a good amount of poetry in this issue, including two new contributors, Kendall Evans and David C. Kopaska-Merkel. Many thanks and hugs go out to all the authors, poets, and illustrators who contributed to the magazine.

Good news department: Michael De Stefano's *American Odyssey* is next to go live, hopefully in the spring. He writes coming-of-age stories about teenagers as they mature into adulthood. Along the way, there's lots of comedy and, alas, some tragedy.

"Night Gallery" will continue with Lee Clark Zumpe reviewing movies. He'll be doing movie reviews for the next forthcoming issues. I'm personally excited to watch some of these movies when I get the time, and I'm sure you'll enjoy his insightful reviews.

I've avoided the shed since the last issue. It's been too cold to go outside unless I'm at the store chasing balloons. If I get enough balloons to enable me to float, I'll tie them around my waist, then venture back to the shed to see if the rags are still there. Last time, I saw the rag pile move, and then I took off before I could see what it was. I'll see what it is this time, but remain afloat and out of reach of whatever is lurking there. I'll wear nose plugs to defuse the odor.

While I'm staying safe inside my house for now, I can imagine the intriguing and mysterious events that unfold during the night. The result of these musings is what you see between the pages. I hope you find comfort and enjoyment in these stories!

IT CAME FROM INSIDE THE INKWELL! By Vincent Davis

"THIS YEAR I'M GOING TO DEVELOP A GOOD RELATIONSHIP
WITH MY BODY...PARTS."

Gone
by
Sandy DeLuca

First time Devin saw me, he gave up a subtle nod, on that sultry night, when bell-bottom jeans and long hair were in style. Kids out on a Friday night, live bands, and drinking from frosted glasses. Sneaking inside the club with a fake ID, dancing with boys who came home from the war. And he watched, older, wiser than me. Tall and somber, shy like me.

On my twenty-first birthday, I drank too much beer, slipped him my number, was crushed because he didn't call. Wasn't until the new year when I saw him again, black hair, blue eyes, Irish kid with five brothers … one sister. And on Valentine's Day, he took me out and kissed me like no one before. All winter, we dated, and he proposed in April. We'd live in the city, have a kid … maybe two. But he was gone by June. Gone with his friends, to parties on the beach … to fast girls and long hot nights smoking pot, singing along with the Stones.

I drove forty miles, found him sitting by the shore, toasting the day with a motley crew. He followed me over the sand back home. And in the fall, I wore his ring again, and January brought parties, him by my side. After work, his old car, dim taillights, puttering down the street, cutting through twilight, there for me when I got off work. My kiss wasn't enough for him, and he left me for a wild girl.

I hit the road, stopping at roadside diners, skipping out without paying the bill. Driving to Miami, high on speed, a dark-eyed guide at my side—one that I never loved. Yet, he taught me magic, how to speak to the dead … and angels on full moon nights. There were others, drifters, seers, tattooed guys, and once a bookshop owner … but none broke my heart like Devin.

Years later, he came back, still loving me despite all the mistakes. He offered security, shelter … his love. I wanted more than he could give. I wanted to make art … tame the elements … fly away on a witch broom … to be free. Then, I was gone, moved to New York, wrote him once. No second thoughts. The hurt was equal; both of us cut each other. I never found another … not like him. Only men who made no promises. And the decades flew by. He never married but had a companion, a drinking partner who enabled his demise.

Me, I sold my art on the sidewalk, rubbed elbows with raggedly vendors, lived with four cats, paid the bills every month. Made offerings … at Esbats, on Sabbats.

January … it brings back his memory. The snow and cold … his arms around me, carrying smoky dreams. And I dreamed I heard that old car's motor … on the night he died.

And he watches … he waits … shadow man out of the corner of my eye … when I splash paint on canvas, when color and form manifests white ghosts, images of those long gone.

Each midnight, that car engine grows louder.

I shudder as snow spirals outside, headlights cut through twilight, subtle nod.

Through destiny, to circle around again.

The End

Cold Future by Sandy DeLuca

Psychedelic jacket,
velvet patches--
bellbottom jeans...
still in vogue

Snow glazes Bleecker Street
as the city stretches out
like a barefaced harlot

Her wrists aglow with rhinestone bracelets;
skull tattoos grin and wrap tortuous
fingers round her ankles

She strains a panhandle smile
with paintings tucked beneath her chin.
bats eyelashes at passersby

No one stops...
so, she plucks a green pill from her pocket,
swallows, and then flicks a switch

The time machine rumbles...
rocks slightly,
then goes back to 1973

Crypt of the Dead Queen by Matthew Wilson

The night has come and all is sound
Now undead things disturb the ground
The chill of ugly moonlight hits the lake
And the fall of men is now at stake.

A chorus of wolves on grass once green
Stained by the blood of a hunter's scream
Cobweb closed are paths between the trees
Yellowed bark withered by witches' disease.

Too soon sunlight will erase this beautiful night
And bleach heroes' bones who lost their might
But now mist collects round this castle keep
In the crypt of which my dead queen sleeps.

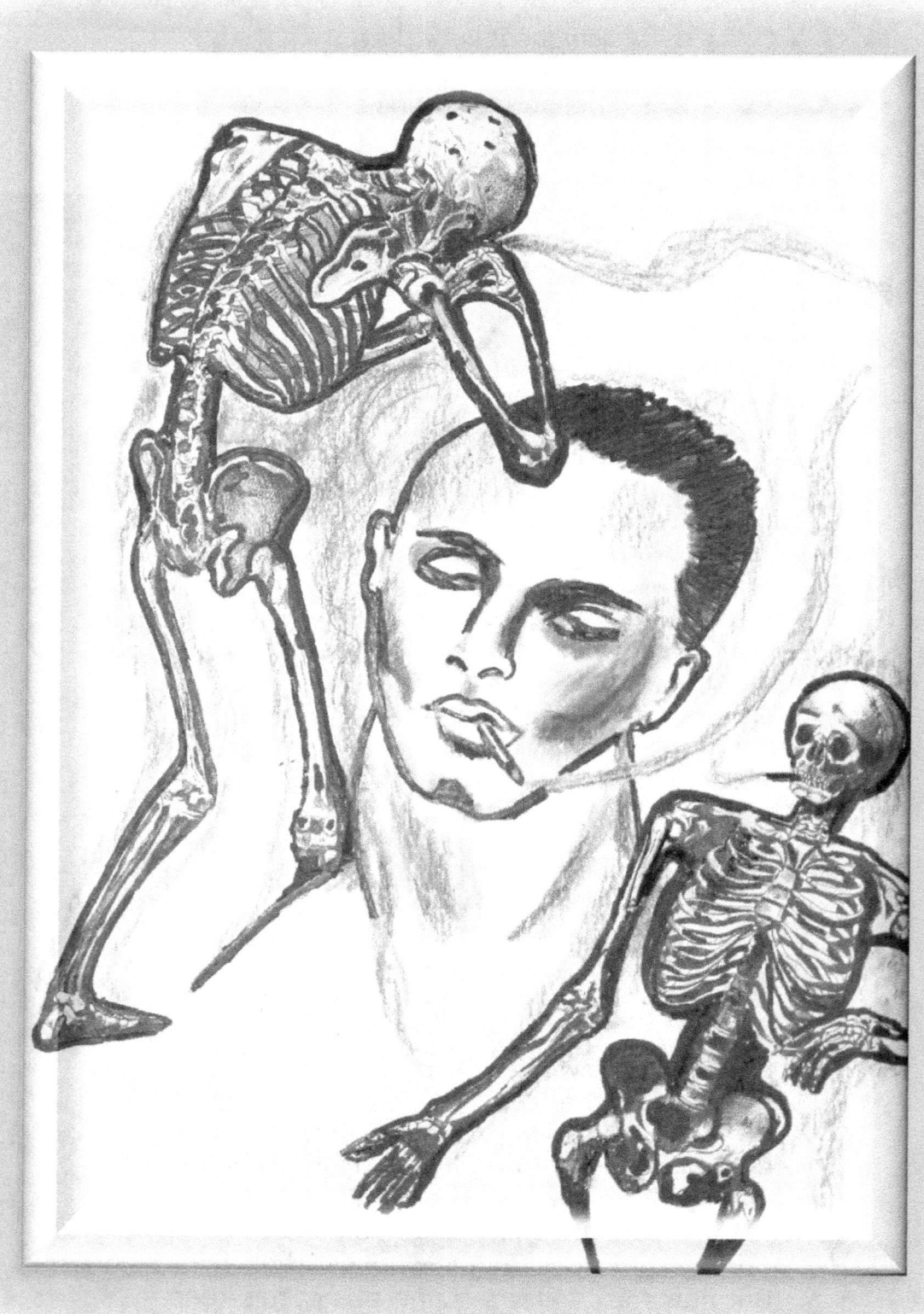

A Message Sent to the Patient Heavens
by
Lee Clark Zumpe

The transmission washed up on our shore like a bottled message drifting in the sea. The first to receive and decode it, the Global Security Administration, probably would have kept it from the public had private organizations and commercial ventures not been involved. Something so historically significant could not have remained classified information for any length of time.

If nothing else, the intercepted signal proved that other civilizations exist in the cosmos. We had already concluded this for ourselves, of course, but this provided hard evidence. Much to the surprise of world governments, leading psychologists, and paranoid theologians, the discovery did not immediately lead to anxious street riots, mass hysteria, or the abandonment of religion. Nervous accounts of alleged alien abductions neither increased nor decreased, and no one set out to arm the world against the threat of an extraterrestrial invasion.

Science did, however, find itself amid a much-needed renaissance. Technologies had to be brought up to speed to explore the possibility that ours was one of the planets mentioned in the transmission.

According to the transmission, hundreds of worlds had been colonized shortly after the dawn of our cosmic time by a highly advanced alien race. The colonization had not taken the form of settling worlds with members of the existing species; but, by introducing single-celled life onto a barren planet—to see what might eventually evolve.

Each of these worlds received a single satellite—a manufactured moon containing concealed monitoring equipment and learning facilities to be accessed by any life form capable of striking out into space. As the transmission put it, "Any race of cognizant beings with a sufficient capacity for knowledge may eventually discover their own origin and employ the limitless resources we have entrusted to them."

We hoped to find a constructive little care package stashed beneath the surface of our moon—a birthday present from our distant benefactors.

I was a member of the first team to reach the moon. The message provided specific instructions on how to locate and access the lunar base. We set down near the rim of the Eratosthenian crater named Picard. As part of the conservative North American consortium—a group that always valued safety and discretion over blind acts of bravado—we spent the first several days on the moon's surface collecting data without leaving the relative comfort of our landing craft. We relayed images and information back to Earth as necessary, most of it unencrypted and available to any one of a dozen different research teams. We broadcasted updates daily through various media outlets, informing the public of our progress.

Of course, we did have a few secrets. We reported our more monumental advances on a secure channel directly to our mission control center in Alaska. By this time, some rifts had emerged among traditional political factions on Earth. While the original transmission had reinforced the ever-strengthening concept of global community, the implications for future development made some people on Earth wary. With only a handful of nations capable of putting astronauts on the moon—and fewer still prepared to do it quickly—suspicion and envy became international pastimes.

In the end, it became a friendly competition to see who could capture the prize first. No one doubted that all humanity would benefit from the discovery—but only one country would have the good fortune of delivering the goods back to the expectant masses of an over-crowded planet.

Unofficially, though, the rivalry ran deep. Distrust vented itself in minor skirmishes—little wars broke out in remote parts of the world. Alliances grew strained, and old animosities flared anew. Vast labor pools in developing countries, jealous of the promise of instant gratification for the elite, threatened to strike unless agreements could be reached.

It was no surprise, then, that within a week of our arrival, two additional contenders had joined us. One originated from the oil-rich Middle Eastern nations. It carried representatives from several countries and pledged to share equally in any breakthroughs. We kept in constant contact with this party, and put aside any enmity that might have soured our mission. We forged friendships, and asked that our supporters on Earth might do the same.

The other ship had been launched from a small island in the Pacific. No one knew who had funded the mission nor who might be aboard the landing craft. Though my team repeatedly tried to make contact with the vessel, we could not convince them to reveal themselves.

After more than a week of sitting along the edge of the crater, probing its depths with our sensors, we felt comfortable taking the next step. Our Middle Eastern counterparts might not have been as prepared, but they refused to let us win all the glory. We welcomed their company, and we descended into the crater.

Even with our advanced jet packs and redesigned spacesuits, the journey down to the floor of Picard took considerable time and energy. Our suits proved more maneuverable than those of the Middle Easterners, and on more than one occasion, we had to assist them when one of their instruments malfunctioned. We had to send one of our team members back to the landing craft when his communicator failed; two members of the Middle Eastern team accompanied him, complaining of difficulty breathing the fabricated air in their masks.

Four of us made it to the door on the floor of the crater. Picard, a small crater found in the northwestern quadrant of Mare Crisium, stretches about fourteen miles in diameter. The gateway constructed by our distant ancestors took up the greater part of the crater's floor. It opened abruptly—practically at the flip of a switch. The speed and fluidity of the mechanism overwhelmed us, and we shuddered at the vastness of it all.

I remember feeling a sweeping nausea overtake me upon seeing the mammoth scale of their technology. I staggered and shook as the immense door slid away beneath my feet, revealing an engineering marvel hidden beneath the surface of the moon. From our vantage point, it seemed that the moon was hollow—and that its interior consisted over layer upon layer of circuitry—vast networks of cables and wires machines and gadgetry that had no recognizable purpose.

Just as we prepared to enter the facility, I saw them: Members of the third landing party had leaped off the rim of the crater and were spiraling down toward us. They employed a compact propulsion device that gave them speed and precision that we could not match. I saw a blinding splash of color to my right, followed rapidly by short bursts of laser fire and additional explosions. I recognized the weapons they carried—weapons I had only seen in my own country, constructed by our military establishment.

The Middle Easterners scrambled for cover inside the mammoth facility. My partner took a hit, and I watched him die, watched him howl inside his spacesuit in the instant before explosive decompression sent his molecules jetting into space.

I pressed myself against the wall of the crater, hoping our assailants would be too eager to explore the facility to bother with me. Either they lost sight of me in their recklessness, or they decided I was no longer an obstacle. They raced down into the soft blue light radiating from the doorway and plunged into the mouth of the lunar base, leaving me to claw at the lip of the Picard crater as I tried to pull myself back to my landing craft.

It must have taken hours to return to the ship.

Once there, I tried to report what had happened to the mission control center. I tried to contact the voracious media correspondents who had relished their daily interviews with me and my crew. No one responded.

I gathered from sporadic reports that the events that had transpired on the moon had been monitored from Earth and had precipitated a major world war. From the periodic flashes of light I saw shimmering on the surface of Earth as I returned from my mission, I guessed that there had been at least a limited nuclear exchange.

That I and my crew even made it back to the orbiting space station was astonishing—but no one on Earth took notice.

With war raging on almost every continent, everyone lost interest in the lunar facility.

In the end, the joke was on us, anyway.

The promise of unlimited resources stockpiled on the moon by an ancient alien race was less than accurate.

I came home empty-handed, obviously; so did everyone else who put a team on the moon to explore the base. Not one task force turned up a trace of helpful information. No one found the so-called Holy Grail that had been guaranteed in the transmission.

No, but we did manage to activate an alien beacon that almost immediately began sending signals out across the cosmos, signals evident to every scanning device here on Earth—signals that indicate a form of life has developed on the planet that was physically and intellectually capable of reaching a nearby satellite and flipping a switch; signals that a race had sufficiently evolved from its single-celled precursors—that it was ready to meet its destiny.

Like a timer buzzing in the kitchen signaling that supper is ready, the moon continues to broadcast our achievement to the patient heavens.

I suspect that the aliens are already on their way.

The End

Shopping for Mom by Matthew Wilson

Bottle of milk
Box of cereal
Eye of newt.

Lady of the Castle
by
Matthew Wilson

At night, I go to the castle because my parents are poor and need the money. The men with swords don't want to bother with the old woman, but someone has to keep her company; someone has to listen to her stories, and so they throw a few coins my way to sit by the hole in the wall where they push in her food.

I have yet to see her, and maybe that won't ever happen. With what she tells me, maybe that is best.

I wish my father would not gamble away the change I bring back. I wish I didn't have to go to the castle again and listen to the old woman forever sealed behind that wall.

To me she has entrusted her life story so it does not turn to dust with her.

I do not want it.

She was beautiful in youth, and though the drunk guards giggle and splash wine on her portrait, I think those deep and loving eyes belong to another person. Someone who has not told me the same stories she whispers through that hole which guards push mush through.

She is *not* allowed knives or forks. Nothing sharp, except her tongue.

I'm scared to dream because she has put demons in my head I never knew existed. Horrible tortures that she delighted in her youth and, though I wake up screaming, Father needs his gambling money.

Mother said it's best to keep the peace for what harm can an old woman do? Mother will be old one day, and she will need taking care of.

I doubt she will tell me stories of the iron maiden or of the many disappearances of her serving girls.

So the guards say winter is soon, and she will be dead. Something so wicked could not survive in those unheated walls during a cold spell, and Father worries about losing his golden egg. I doubt the Devil could kill the lady of the castle.

Maybe he could visit this Lady Bathory instead.

The End

Vampire Aliens by Denny E. Marshall

two-hundred-year pass
UFO returns for him
vampire boards ship

vampire killer
almost caught by the police
Makes way to spacecraft

Leaving the City by Marge Simon

Too long I've languished here,
I miss my kindred --
Not the Undead here,
Thriving in the city lights,
Clubbing off Broadway
My pretentious sisters
Six days a week
Professing innocence
And on the Sabbath,
Despite the pomp and ritual,
just as needy
for the juice of life as I

When I return
To the blue mountains,
I'll don my homespun robe,
Commune with honest ravens
On old stone walls.

Do Not Touch My Computer!
by
Rod Marsden

Garry Evans was a middle-aged man with little knowledge of family life outside his own sibling and her husband and children. He was on his own most of the time. Hoping to change that, he decided to share a house with a woman about his age and her son. Splitting every expense from rent to electricity would be fine. She seemed nice, and her son was polite when they first met, so he thought everything would be all right.

The woman's name was Julie, and her son's name was Tim. The son was a tall sixteen then and turned out to be an annoyance for Garry. He complained about how Garry washed up in the kitchen after a meal. Was the water too cold, and why didn't he wear gloves and use hot water? It got so bad that Garry ate out of cans or went out for takeaway.

Moreover, after a long trip on the train after work, Garry wanted some time on his computer, a television program, a book, and his bed. This was all frustrated when he received a knock on the door from Tim. It would happen every afternoon after his computer made the start-up sound. If he ignored the knocking, it would turn into a pounding, so he had to open his bedroom door. What followed was a dreary conversation he could have lived without.

One day, he got to the house, and there was a hole in the wall near his bedroom. Tim had kicked it in, and Julie said she would have it mended at her own expense. This she did. Also, there was the question of a hot shower. He felt anyone was entitled to this, but Tim, turning on all the taps in the house, ensured his showers ran cold instead. On another occasion, he broke into Garry's room and riffled through his stuff. Julie slapped him hard and made him apologise for this, but it was too much. Garry had to get out. He hadn't realised this before, but he was a man of routines and could barely function without them. He hated living in chaos.

Julie always paid her share of the rent and electricity late. He covered for her for a few months. She always paid him back, but because of this, Garry had difficulty saving. In the end, he told Julie he was moving out. She was not happy about this, and neither was her son. Garry would have moved if not for an accident that occurred when he was crossing the road to get to work. The previous night, he had been drinking to make up for not being able to enjoy his computer, his television set, his book, and his bed. Hence, he was dazed and not looking where he was going when a truck smacked into him. At this juncture, Julie owed him four hundred dollars. He died, but that was not the end of him as far as Julie and Tim were concerned.

Tim claimed the computer among the things in Garry's room. Garry's relatives got everything else except the computer and the television set. The story was that the computer and television set were broken and thrown away. They thought this was bunk but let it go. They had arranged to help Garry move and had some inkling as to why he needed to do so.

The computer's start-up sound was different. It was like a banshee's wail before acting like a normal computer. Tim initially found this to be cool. Then, the machine sent emails to his teachers, peer students, and parents of students in his school, outlining the bullying he had done over the years. The sender was G for Garry. There were other bullies in his school, but they preferred a less prominent profile. Thus, they ignored him in the playground and after school. When he confronted three of them, they beat him up. For once, it was Tim coming home with bruises and not one of his victims. The kids he forced to do his homework for him made it clear that this would no longer happen since they now had their parents, teachers, and principal backing them. He had to study with his mother helping out on rare occasions. It was barely enough to get by academically. Moreover, he spent more time in detention to make up for past crimes.

There was now something wrong with the television set stolen from Garry. It would play nothing but ads. The shower was also a bother. It would spray nothing but cold water. Even an electrician couldn't figure out why. Getting someone to pay the other half of the rent proved difficult because of Tim's worsening reputation. So, they had to move to a small unit where rent was more affordable. Even so, the stolen television set only played ads in the new place, and the new shower would only produce cold water. The water at the kitchen sink was always scalding hot.

One day, when Tim was at the school library, a heavy book flew off a shelf and hit him in the back of the head. He turned around, but no one was there. He thought he heard someone snigger. "It's a dictionary, you idiot," came a whisper from nearby. His mother wondered about the lump on his head, but he couldn't say how he got it. He was embarrassed at being hit by a book.

On Tim's last day at high school, he was ganged up on and punched by a dozen boys and girls he had earlier tormented. When he got home, he thought about searching the internet to find something to watch to ease that day's pain. This time, the start-up sound was the one he heard when Garry owned the computer. It was followed by a polite knock on the door to his bedroom. He called out, but it wasn't his mother. "Who is it?" he cried. There was no reply. Then, the knocking got louder and louder. Suddenly, the door burst open, and a great wind assailed Tim. It was hot as if it had been issued from Hell. When it stopped, Tim wanted to think nothing of it. He needed it to be just his imagination, but he had trouble convincing himself that this was so. The computer went back to just being a computer.

A year later, Tim got a job in a warehouse. To do stock, he had to use Excel on the warehouse computer. There seemed to be nothing wrong with what he was doing, but overnight, something tampered with the settings, and the inventory was off by large amounts of stock. Items ordered in the warehouse weren't needed, and urgent items had been cancelled. All this had Tim's warehouse code attached, so it was apparent he was responsible for this mess. He was fired, and word went out so other warehouses would not hire him. His mother could not help him as he slipped more and more into destitution and then drunkenness.

It seemed computers were no longer friendly toward Julie, so she had difficulty holding down a job. Eventually, mother and son went their separate ways. At an ATM one day, Julie put in her bank card and punched in a request for a couple of hundred dollars. Instead of money, she got two IOUs for two hundred dollars. She marched into the bank with the IOUs for an explanation, but then the IOUs turned into the two hundred dollars she was expecting. Hence, the cashier didn't know what her problem was. She took to drink, wondering when the nightmare she was experiencing would end.

A week after the IOU incident, Tim started up the stolen computer to see if he could find a job somewhere. Without skills and a bad warehouse history, he was desperate to find something. There was nothing for him, so he went to a pawn shop with the computer the following day. He tried to get money for it, but that was no good. He didn't have proof he owned it, and the guy behind the counter wasn't interested in stolen merchandise. He returned the computer to the bedsitter he rented and wondered what his next move should be. He was behind on rent and couldn't get on the dole for some reason. Government websites refused to acknowledge his existence. His birth certificate was not acknowledged by the hospital where he was born, and he had never had a driver's license.

"Who am I?" Tim asked himself as he bumped into a pub, stole and drank some beers, and was thrown out. He tried to return to his bedsitter but was locked out. The computer and some of his other belongings were beside the door. He thought to ring his mother but didn't have a phone. He was ragged, and he smelled. People on the street avoided him. His belongings included a duffle bag, bedroll, spare shoes, a toothbrush and paste, and that damnable computer. A member of the Salvation Army found him trying to keep warm in his blanket on a park bench and took him to where he could get something to eat and have a place to sleep.

The computer came to life sometime in the night, spraying him with images of his past. These included banging the door to disturb Garry Evans, turning hot water cold by opening taps throughout the house, and other misdeeds. He wondered how he could be shown anything since the computer was unplugged. Then, a hand holding a book reached out from the screen, and the book flew at him, hitting him on the face. Tim screamed and ran. He found a window, jumped out, and was hit by a truck.

The police report was a no-brainer. Due to experiencing vivid nightmares because of alcoholism, Tim had run from night terrors into the path of the vehicle that ended his existence. The truck driver was not at fault. They were able to trace Tim's mother via his birth certificate, which now was acceptable, and give her the news of his passing. The Salvation Army gave the police the computer, which was eventually given to Gary's family via the serial number, where it performed tasks like a regular computer. Julie had dumped Gary's television set years ago, but it somehow ended up with the police, and they saw to it that it was taken to Gary's family. It went back to being a regular television set.

After Tim's death, eight hundred dollars went missing from Julie's meagre savings, forcing her to subsist for two weeks on nothing more than tins of baked beans. She remembered owing Garry the four hundred. An extra four hundred made sense for what she and her son had put him through. Then, the shade that had tormented Julie ceased to do so for a while, and she could return to the workforce. She came to prefer to work where she didn't have much to do with computers. Even so, her pay had to go into her bank account, and she had to use an ATM to get any of it out. It seemed that getting completely away from computers was impossible. She just had to hope that, from now on, they would be nice to her.

A decade later, she passed away in a sleazy apartment in a disreputable part of the city. The eight hundred dollars that had gone missing reappeared in her bank account and was whisked away to Gary's sister's account. It was the final act of the ghost of Garry Evans.

The End

Dark Trinity by Chris Friend

I guard the three places
Where crossroads meet.
I have a face for each path:
One is the fox,
Sly and hungry;
Another is the cat,
All chaos and night;
Last is the owl,
Merciless as death and winter.
I am a phantom
Bloody with scabs;
I am lord to the shadows
And will not carry the clutter,
Except for the keys to Hell,
For I hold the secrets
Of the damned and doomed.

Winter Company by Chris Friend

A great wash tub
Of a woman
Who'd hunted bears
With a switch

Stirs the kettle
As the train passes
And rattles
The bones of bears
And old men

Stashed away
In the closet
They wait
To be pulled out
As company
For those long winter months

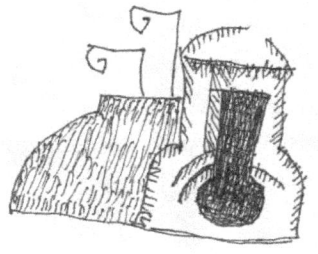

Chasing the Ragged Flag
by
Hillary Lyon

His breath was a ragged flag snapping in the cold wind.

I could see it, even in this dim twilight. Pale, undulating, edges frayed, moving farther away with each step. He was fast, but I was faster. After sprinting less than a mile through these sparse woods, he slowed. His flag heaved and fluttered.

As he leaned against a tall, thin tree to catch his breath, his heartbeat was a beacon in the burgeoning night. Flashing red, alternately flaring and dimming, leading me right to him. I got on my knees and watched from a thicket.

I crawled closer.

Overhead, the moon made her appearance behind high, thin clouds. Around his head, a handful of fireflies now orbited, gifting him a halo of tiny green and yellow stars.

He was a destination on a crumpled map, circled in blinking neon.

He gasped. Did he hear me approach? Did I step on a twig or rustle a cluster of low branches? Did I carelessly crunch a dry leaf underfoot? Perhaps he was stifling a sob; such unbridled emotions these hikers exude—they send waves and ripples of feelings that wash over me like a warm bath. I lap the air with my slender, prehensile tongue and taste the salty-sweet flavor of his panic and desperation. My stomach rumbled.

His head jerked up; he scanned the stars, looking for a familiar constellation—any constellation—to guide him back to civilization. I drifted up, as silent as smoke, fog, or what-have-you, to roost on a bare limb directly overhead.

My eyes were owl eyes, seeing everything cloaked by the darkness of night: the quivering little mammals in their burrows, the stealthy predators prowling through the underbrush. The trembling, fatigued creature cowering beneath my perch.

Aroused by his fear and despair, long, strong, sharp talons formed on my fingertips. My fangs pushed through the tender flesh of my gums.

Now glittering, my body expanded. I filled the sky, covering the stars with my own constellations. My breath swirled around him, funneling gritty, dry debris and the sweet, perfumed dust of desiccated wildflowers. His internal compass spun wildly; he was lost.

In the growing chill, his breath punched from his gaping mouth in irregular puffs. His flag now wavered weakly and drooped, signaling the game was almost over.

Unable to navigate this situation, much less comprehend it, he was deliciously vulnerable. Like aged beef, now that he was properly seasoned, he was savory—ripe and juicy with fear. My mouth watered at the thought.

Follow me, I whispered, sending slender aural tendrils to twine about his neck, to caress his face, to ruffle his hair. In his ears, my voice was an atonal melody from a sea-glass windchime gently fingered by a curious breeze. *I will take you home.*

Oh, how his heart filled with relief and joy. That meaty pump brimmed with hope inside its cage of chalky bone—a frail cage whose lock I would later pick with ease. After this harrowing chase, this exhausting game of hide and seek, he was, at last, going home—

Though I never specified *whose* home.

****

They're advertised as kennels, but they're just large cages. I don't care for them; I don't like the idea of any creature forced to live in a cramped, cold little wire prison. so I allow my quarry to roam freely on my property. I believe this keeps them healthier, less stressed, and decidedly happier, as being uncaged gives them hope. *Hope of what?* you wonder. Hope of escaping, obviously,

But do they ever run away or wander off? Not as long as I have them dosed with my glamour. Eyes wide, they see nothing but twinkling stars overhead and a beautiful verdant forest around them. Periodically, the sweet smell of wildflowers on a warm breeze wafts over them, carrying the enchanted dust of my glamour. They breathe deeply and are becalmed.

This is a most ethical treatment. If not *the* most.

And when their time comes—or I should say, when my hunger roars deep within me like the ravening demon it is, demanding to be unshackled and set loose in the world to chase the ragged flag waving before them—then we play a game reminiscent of hide and seek. You surely remember that childhood amusement. In my version, they hide in what they think are shadow-dense woods—when in reality, they are cowering in the middle of my sparsely treed yard. As the seeker, I growl and crawl in ever-shrinking circles around them. They tremble and whimper. Knowing what comes next, the full moon hides her bright face behind a thick veil of clouds.

It's over in a matter of minutes.

Unlike my brethren, I refuse to callously toss the remains in the garbage, burn them in a pile of leaves and refuse, or dump them in a shallow grave. That is *so* very disrespectful, and I am all about respecting the creatures of the natural world, even if I will never be one.

Instead, I prefer to honor my prey, especially after I'm done with them. Come with me, and I'll show you.

I'll unlock the door to my private, ah, study. Few of your kind have experienced the privilege of entering this room. Don't shudder, don't dread what awaits inside! Save that fear for other, more—*deadly*—encounters.

See there, to the right of my stone-cold fireplace, the dozens of heads mounted on the wall? Each one lovingly cleaned, coiffed, and touched up with the best mortuary makeup. Note how the moonlight streaming through the bay window paints delicate shadows on their faces, giving them the illusion of life's emotional expressions. Observe how some look happy, some surprised, some wary, some frightened, some bored. This wall is a veritable cavalcade of stories! It's better than television.

And there, on the top row, in the farthest corner—note the ornately carved oak plaque, bare and waiting for the next head. Patiently waiting for my next prized trophy.

Waiting for *you*.

The End

Back Up
by
Marc Shapiro

Fred could not believe his eyes. There he was, minding his own business, wandering the aisles at F Stop Market, scoping out deodorant when he rounded a corner…

That's when he saw her. What he saw was her back. What he saw was magic.

Fred was a leg man, but this was insanity. It was legs up to here, sculpted to well-muscled perfection, all the way up to there. There were black, skin-tight short shorts where the legs disappeared. Fred could find nothing out of place. The tight white shirt was a joy to behold, the long, straight, black hair making a beeline for the middle of her back. She was taller than tall in the most entrancing, enticing way.

Fred had stumbled upon heaven or was he tempted by the possibility of hell.

As he stepped slightly to the right, to better to catch her from the front, the more surprised, shocked, and frustrated he was. All he continued to see was her back in all its glory, doing the body dance of perfection as she rounded the corner and sauntered down the next aisle.

Fred followed at a distance, a bulldog in heat, ogling every square inch of her bodily bliss. He circled around, hoping to see the face that would launch a thousand ardor ships. But once again, all he saw was body, butt, legs, and hair. Fred could have watched what he was seeing forever. But damn it! That face must have been the cat's meow, and he was beginning to lose his composure at what he was dying to see. His imagination slipped into overdrive. Was this vision something not of this earth?

Fred did a sudden shuck and jive to the right. He was seemingly within sight. This would be the money vision. But all he could see was her backside, which continued a grand spectacle but nothing more.

Fred pulled out the heavy artillery.

He yelled at her. The vision stopped and turned to face him. It was the same on the other side. The second side of the same posterior he had seen. Fred's mind was now officially blown. He took cautious steps back. What could this vision be? A thing from another world with no face dropped into the aisles of F Stop Market to torture earthling horn dogs?

He had to know.

The body nonchalantly paid for its purchases and exited the store. If the checker was getting the full picture, he wasn't saying. Not too far behind in hot pursuit, Fred lost his cool and screamed out:

"Let me see your face! Damn it! What do you look like? Show me the complete package!"

The body stopped cold. Hesitated a moment and turned to face Fred, who lost it. What he finally saw was a complete blank slate. No eyes. No nose. No ears. Fred gasped. All he could see were fangs.

As they lurched forward and bit into his jugular.

The End

Crazy Than Thou by Marc Shapiro

I am crazy
You are not
But who is one to believe
The one who commits the foul deed
The one who gets off on the telling
Or the one whose trophies of the kills
Hang proudly around the neck
Where does the answer lay
It may be the one
Who inflicts the bloody violence
The death by a thousand sharp fangs
Or the one who glories in the shivers
It's up to you and to me
To determine the truth
And just who is the monster
In all of us
Ready to rend and tear

Before I Do It Again by Marc Shapiro

Stop me
Before I bleed again
The thoughts
The vile scenarios
They fall like raindrops
From a darkening sky
Stop me
Because I am the monster
The source of all insanity
I don't know where it comes from
I don't know where it's been
But it's here now
Driving me to madness
I only have one hope
Please stop me
Before I write again

Date Night
by
Hal Kempka

"I met a girl the other night on my pizza delivery route," Darren said. "She is one hot bitch, the kind I could really sink my teeth into."

His friend Jonathan sat on the bar stool beside him in the Green Onion Lounge. "Oh yeah? What does she look like?"

"Her name is Carrie Ann, and she's a grad student here at the university. She is short, has great hooters, and has pitch-colored hair. Dude, she's got these dark, mysterious eyes that draw you to her. They are fucking mesmerizing and seem to drill right through you."

"What's her major?"

"Forensic Science. She is taking some night classes to finish her credits this semester."

"Oh, buddy, if she's who I think she is, you'd better get out of that relationship fast."

"Why?"

"Man, I heard she dates men like eating sunflower seeds; chews them up and spits them out."

"Nah, she's not like that at all," Darren said, shaking his head. "In fact, when I delivered the pizza, she invited me to come back after I finished work. I did, and we spent the night together. I'm telling you, she's a firecracker in bed."

"Just the same, be careful, man. I don't want to see you getting your heart ripped out like that blonde did to you two semesters ago. It took you most of the summer to get out of your depression."

"Well, I'm not letting that happen. Tell you what; I am meeting up with her in a while. I'll see if she has a friend, and we'll swing by. Maybe we can party hardy, my man."

"I might, but don't count on it. If I'm still here when you come by, then we will party like it's 1999."

As the night wore on, Jonathan decided to take Darren up on his offer. He waited at the bar for Darren and his new girlfriend. When they failed to show, he shivered, and his concern compelled him to call Darren's cell. It went right to voice mail.

His friend never said he would do something and not follow it through. Jonathon drove to the house where he said Carrie Ann lived. His friend's car was parked along the curb in front of the house, and he pulled to the curb behind it.

Tall palms and yellowish path lights dotted the ice plants edging the long, winding walkway. He glanced around, checking for any neighbors who might be out. Seeing none, he followed the secluded walkway. Spreading Birds of Paradise plants partially hid the house from the street.

Jonathan crept into the shadows between two of the huge bushes. He peered through the darkness into the dimly lit living room. After watching for several minutes and seeing nothing, he started back toward his car

A dim light shining through another window toward the back of the house caught his eye. He crept up and peeked in. He scanned the room and spotted Darren with his feet protruding from one end of loveseat that faced a brick fireplace. He appeared to be banging with his girl-friend, whose naked back rose and fell above the couch in a steady rhythm.

He watched for several more minutes. Carrie Ann rose from the couch and ran her fingers through her disheveled, thick, and shiny Onyx hair. She grabbed a handful of tissues and wiped away smeared lipstick from her mouth.

She giggled and walked from the room. The dim light shining through her black gossamer gown outlined her curvy, broad hips and trim waistline. Darren had certainly been right about her being wonderfully endowed, and Jonathan felt a twinge of desire flood through him.

A moment later, she returned, carrying a wineglass. She glanced down toward Darren and smiled, saying something to him that Jonathan could not make out. She then knelt in front of the couch, and out of sight.

A few minutes later, Carrie Ann stood and looked toward the window. She raised her glass to her lips, gulping the contents, not bothering to wipe away the thick red liquid dripping off her lips and onto her chin.

She reached down and lifted Darren's severed head. Blood dripped from his friend's head into her glass, and Jonathan stood paralyzed with fear. She looked toward the window and smiled at Jonathan. His feet felt cinder block heavy as he stepped back from the window into the shadows.

Jonathan turned to run when Carrie Ann swept across the room toward him. Her body glowed in a strange translucence, and her shiny black hair flowed behind her with the wildness of an angry horse. She seemed to shapeshift as she floated through the house wall toward him.

He stumbled toward his car, fumbling through his pockets for the car keys. Searing pain shot through his back, and he gasped with a hoarse whisper that was intended to be a scream. He collapsed to the pavement.

Carrie Ann floated above him momentarily before kneeling beside him. She held his heart in her hands and smiled motherlike. After she wiped it across his lips, the organ quivered with a dying beat. She lifted it to her lips and bit into it as if it were a ripened apple.

After cradling him in her arms, she retreated toward the house, emitting a sardonic shriek that sliced through the darkness like a hot, high-pitched desert wind. Jonathon's corpse glowed from her translucence, and he never felt the drops of his blood that dripped from her chin and onto his cheeks.

The End

Their Impeccable Pedigree by Lee Clark Zumpe

The bloodline has been much diluted
across the span of centuries –
their rather irresponsible attitude
resulted in an infinite variety of breeds,
and a gradual loss of purpose.

Still, one House remained uncorrupted
throughout the chronicle of civilization –

their impeccable pedigree
maintained by loyal disciples
in exchange for wealth and power.

The earliest forebears were worshipped
in the forgotten cities of Ophir and Ulthar –
their uncanny perception
earning the hearts and souls
of their lumbering devotees.

Now, the House of Bastet pulls the strings
from shadowy, secreted lairs and hidden halls –
their prophetic intuition
filtered through faithful zealots
dictating the course of history.

The Fox Man by Todd Hanks

Once his human form had changed
the Fox Man found himself chased,
running in his red fox shape.

For the fox in the glen
the new blue of the night
was a cloak and within
was a place he could hide
from the hounds on his trail
that were howling behind.

He then crossed at a stream
that was silver and green.
When the bugle was faint
the Fox Man took a break
and it hid in a log.
Then he longed for his mate
in the growth of the fog.

Restrained... by Denny E. Marshall

Restrained cannot budge
the fear is thick as
person on conveyor belt
ahead of you drops into
the blood covered wood chipper

A Carnival of Ghosts
by
Marge Simon

So there was an argument about something, you forget what. Wife took the car, fled to her mother, or maybe you dropped her off; you can't be sure, but never mind. Now here you are, a free man with nothing planned on a warm summer night pulsing with excitement; a carnival has come to town.

You enter the gate, expecting the rush of joy you knew as a boy, but you're met instead with a discordant roar in your ears that makes your mind recoil. The Kamikaze ride looms, brightly colored flashing lights, with screams and shrieks of passengers; wild thrills in twirling baskets tempt, but no fun alone, you pass it by.

Beneath the cacophony, there is a sense of isolation stabbed by time, defaming Bradbury's gestalt; a magic dark and unsettling, nostalgia by proxy. A carousel of skeletal horses revolves and strobe lights flicker on the palsied faces of the riders, pale hands clutching the poles, bobbing up and down in blissful madness. You are captivated by music from a glittering organ charming the night while faceless vendors vie for attention; a charade of tempting games—hit the baby elephants and swans. Around and around they parade before the sights of your gun. You think you hit them all because the shill hands you a blood-soaked Teddy Bear.

In the Tunnel of Love, your wife is waiting for you in the little boat, but something is wrong with her neck. There is blood on her dress and in her hair. She kisses your hand. You stagger past the wreck of a car—a very familiar car, crumpled outside the entrance to The Hall of Mirrors where you find reflections of yourself in multiples—body under a sheet, toe tag with your name. The raucous laughter isn't yours. There is no exit, this is your last stop, you're just another prisoner in the Carnival of Ghosts.

The End

Journey
by
Linda Barrett

We landed our craft in a place among many trees. A mountain overlooked the road and, and, and it felt cold when we slid out the door. On my craft's side, we encountered a small being with many legs. We made first contact with it and absorbed it. We became one. After we digested the creature, we took on its image and left to explore this area.

We walked in this insect form through fallen trees and under the muddy surface. Winged creatures flew overhead. One swooped down when we came out into the sun. It opened its beak and swallowed us.

We ate through its organs, digesting them, and took host in its body. We flew over the trees and scanned the area for other life forms we would encounter. The bird who devoured us showed me kilometers of trees and a mountain known as Denali. The white material on the ground was called snow.

Our avian host called it Alaska.

Our host, the bald eagle, perched on a branch. We made observations on the vegetation and the atmosphere. It dove into a body of water and swallowed a fish. We dissolved the fish and became one with it. The fish and we fell out of the dead eagle's mouth and swam through the water called a lake. Another fish opened its mouth and devoured us. We made the bigger fish a host and traveled through the river. We jumped and dove alongside a fish called salmon which came to spawn with its own kind.

A metal hook caught in our mouth and pulled us out. We landed on a wooden structure called a dock. A human man wearing a hunter's cap and a puffy vest bent down and picked us up. As he pulled the hook out of our mouth, we absorbed the fish and went through the man's body.

As the man screamed, we absorbed him and took on his image. When we came into his brain, we surmised he was going to eat the fish for his nighttime meal. We took on his nature and eavesdropped on his thoughts.

We rode in his wheeled mechanical vehicle called a jeep along a road, which changed into a highway. He came into a dwelling place made of logs, and his wife embraced him. It was time for me to absorb them. They screamed as we emerged from the man's mouth and into the wife's mouth. I digested them both on their living room floor. We reverted to our original form and slid across their carpet.

Their daughter came down and opened her mouth to scream.

We threw ourselves over her and united with her body.

We looked into her bedroom mirror. She was undergoing a physical transformation called puberty. We felt her skin with all its red and white bumps called acne. She went through a maturation period with emotional difficulties. We ran her fingers down her cheeks to feel her tears. We found a communication device on her vanity under the mirror. We read the images on it. Friends showed pictures of her, describing her in what she called teasing. She rose from her chair, and we found her suitcase. After she put her clothes in it, we snapped the case shut and went down the stairs.

We searched her thoughts.

"Are you expecting someone?" we asked her, acquainted with her language, which she called English.

"Leave me alone!" she said in her anger.

Her communication device registered a boy looking for a girl for a mating relationship. She contacted him on the thing. It was an application for a website that matched adolescents to other adolescents. We scanned her mind to explain whom she was looking for. He was a youth called Tad.

She found his profile, and they planned to run away together.

We discovered her name was Topaz.

"Topaz," we asked. "Will you mate with Tad?"

"I love him," she replied.

"What is love?" we asked.

"You're just as bad as my parents. That's all they talk about. 'You don't love me enough!' my mom says to my dad. He looks at naked women on his tablet while she's not looking. He tells her he's going out with his friends, and they go to the Nome strip club. Why am I telling you this? I need to know what love is before I turn 21. After that, I'm no good. I'm 13, and my biological clock's ticking."

"I only combine with another of my kind." We told her. "We unite and reproduce when we link together. We are part of a one-celled organism."

"Everyone has a boyfriend but me. They've all had sex, and they know how to attract guys."

"Attract a mate?" we asked.

Topaz showed her grief emotion. We felt the hot tears grow cold on her face. We walked alongside the road while vehicles passed by us at great speed. The other humans seemed busy traveling to other destinations on this land called Alaska. We needed to devour another life form for nutrition. We would keep Topaz as a host until the time came.

We went into the state park where the forest was. We stood by the information board.

Tad sat in his vehicle. I registered Topaz's memories of him. Instead of seeing the handsome, clean-cut teenager as on Topaz's phone, my eyes took in a balding man in the middle of his life span.

I sensed he was not the Tad on the phone. His hair was almost gone, and he wore a device that improved his eyesight.

Topaz's nostrils took in an unusual odor of an artificial scent with unwashed flesh. He wore clothes unknown to the men of this Alaska. The men of Alaska wore flannel and denim. This Tad had on bland fabrics and colors. Topaz's mind registered him as a geek. I sensed her revulsion. She seemed disappointed.

"Where's Tad?" she asked when she came to what she called a pick-up truck.

"Oh, he's studying for his exams. Pre-med, you know."

Topaz climbed into the vehicle's passenger side.

"I'm ready to see him," she laughed.

"My name's Trevor," the man said. "I'm Tad's uncle."

****

What happened next made me wonder about colonizing this planet. Trevor showed her around his living space. Together, our minds searched for Tad, only to discover she was with Trevor. He let her sit down in his cluttered apartment. He had reading materials everywhere. His clothing lay on the rotting couches. Our nostrils took in the odor of animal excrement. Scanning Topaz's mind, we realized she was in danger. She was sorely disappointed.

"Where's Tad?" she asked. We shuddered in icy, sudden fear as Trevor came up to us with a knife.

Trevor bound us up in something called duct tape. We drank soda, which made us sleepy. Our minds took information about the sleeping medicine in it. He carried us over his shoulder to the basement, where he had a table with mechanical cutting tools for building houses. Our minds took in the residue of human blood on their jagged blades. Trevor removed our clothing, folding it neatly into a pile along with other girl garments. He tied her to the table in a spread-eagle fashion.

This is where we took our action. Trevor felt his crotch and realized he had to vent his bladder of liquid waste products. He ran upstairs and left Topaz to her doom. Or so it seemed.

Sliding out of her nostrils, we copied her form. Topaz did not respond to us leaving her body due to the fact she was drugged.

Trevor pounded down the stairs, and his mouth opened.

He screamed.

Turning around, we looked at him.

"Why do you want to kill us?" we asked.

Trevor pressed himself up against the basement wall. Our new image was reflected in his greasy glasses.

"Who's the other girl?" he asked.

We came up to him and wrapped our arms around his neck.

"Take me," we commanded him.

Our lips met.

Trevor lay there, still uncomprehending. We united our bodies in human reproduction, but he was not satisfied. He crawled backward and huddled in the corner.

"What are you?" he screamed.

We did not answer. With our teeth, we bit off the ropes from Topaz's wrists. We proceeded to free her. There was no time for words or actions. Trevor sat there, quivering in terror because he could not understand what had happened.

Topaz rose to her feet and looked at us.

"How'd you do that?" she asked.

"We are not of your world. We only came here to reproduce and absorb what we must study."

"Can you take me with you?" Her eyes widened in surprise.

Trevor charged at us with something called a chainsaw. He sliced us through with it, and we became more Topazes. The human Topaz raced upstairs with her clothing. We found ourselves becoming wearier and wearier. Our energy ran out, and we fell to the floor.

Trevor pulled out another sharp weapon, and we only had one last resort to save ourselves. We all merged into Topaz. Trevor stabbed and stabbed at us until we were all apart. We found one of my core members left. There was nothing we could do but surrender.

The police ran down the stairs to find Trevor. He sat there against the basement stairs, his eyes wide and mouth open. They didn't know what they witnessed next, but it was something that would not be believed on their police account.

We slid out of Trevor's nostrils with the rest of my young. We feasted well on his inner organs.

The End

Dragon Scat and Vampire Ash by Kendall Evans and David C Kopaska-Merkel

Eve of newt and mandrake root
Dragon scat and vampire ash—
What better substances to fuel our spaceship?
One uses what one can
modern engines all depend
on elements unknown here
tools that we don't have

The problem is space aliens
who have no world of their own
they make their nests in asteroids
(imagine a giant beehive)—
The have voracious appetites
For any kind of rocket fuel
and they can smell the ingredients
thru the vacuum from lightyears away

toe of frog, tongue of dog
wool of bad and adder's fork
arsenic and old lady's lace
the space aliens crave them all

Interstellar Dreams by Kendall Evans

The Captain and the maintenance AI
are playing an endgame of chess
in the starship's stately lounge

While the stoker again and again
flings shovelfuls of black coal
into the ship's reactor

Inside the reactor everything glows
blue-diamond bright, incandescent
showing every image photons ever told

As Ophelia's pale corpse
drifts past our starship
riding currents of interstellar dust

And the aft constellation depicting a dragon
roars out thunderous gravity waves
as two black holes collide

Only the sorceress onboard the starship
can perceive the low rumble
of gravity's deepest frequencies

She thinks: it's like hearing
the drumbeats and heartbeats
of primitive deities

Wake of the White Death
by
Lee Clark Zumpe

Wimarc Essex approached the planet Celestria with considerable caution.

"Maintain standard orbit," Wimarc said. Lean and angular, the young ship's captain surveyed the ice dwarf, trying to tease out its secrets. "Continue customary arrival declaration, in case someone happens to be listening." He articulated the orders mechanically, knowing his crew needed no instruction. "Aldred," Wimarc said, running through the ordinary post-jump diagnostics, "I'd like to see if we can link with the surveillance cams down there." Savaric Vogel, his seasoned second in command, searched for traces of recent orbital traffic. "And if there are any giant space monsters out there about to make a meal out of my ship, I'd appreciate it if someone would let me know."

The last three envoys dispatched to the colony had simply disappeared. Communications with each of the spacecraft had been severed without any hint of distress. The names of more than three dozen passengers and crew members became file headers in a collection of *Missing in Action* documents stored on a database housed on Gunnora, the region's administrative headquarters and the first Goldilocks planet to be settled more than 10,000 light-years from Earth.

Deep-space scans found no trace of the jump-drive cutters that carried the previous contact teams to Celestria, beginning with the *Rasheed* one Terran year earlier. While the overlords managing the First Trade Coalition on Earth seemed willing to write off the colony, Idonea Haversham, the regional supervisor, had other plans. A blemish on her résumé would impair her chances at future promotion, and she wanted a cushy managerial position overseeing the revitalization of the entertainment complex on Saturn's moon Titan.

Haversham knew, though, that her superiors on Earth would not sanction a fourth formal recovery mission. In their eyes, the significant loss in both personnel and equipment (but mostly equipment) had made the abandonment of the Celestria mining colony obligatory. Any chance at salvage and recuperation would have to come through an atypical and innovative course of action.

Soldier of fortune Wimarc Essex and his so-called Myrmidons won a bidding war for Haversham's lucrative contract. They had arrived in orbit around Celestria within 72 hours of finalizing the deal, completing three separate jumps in Wimarc's Callisto class frigate, *Rattlesnake*.

"I can't access their security systems, chief." Aldred, Wimarc's tech guru, spoke without taking his gaze off the monitors. His face was gaunt, his expression stern. His nimble fingers danced across the control panel as he tried to hack the network in hopes of bypassing authentication and stumbling on a symmetrical backdoor. "I could modify a Trojan horse, but it would take some time."

"We're not staying any longer than necessary," Wimarc said, ruling out an armchair mission. "Aldred, Forwin, and Amiria are with me," the chief announced, naming those who would accompany him to the surface. "Gear up, heavy armor, fully outfitted. Savaric, you have command. Don't let the children get into any trouble." Wimarc's *Rattlesnake* carried a nominal support crew of eight hard-edged adventurers belowdecks who loathed the monotony of being excluded from action. "Anything looks weird to you and you can't reach us, button up and fly home."

"I did find something they didn't notice on Gunnora." Savaric, the team's eldest member, played a digitized code on the loudspeakers as Wimarc and the others prepared to head for one of two shuttlecrafts found on the frigate. "It's a quarantine beacon with a low-power output, only detectable from orbit. I haven't been able to validate the serial number, so I can't tell you who deployed it."

"Probably one of Gunnora's envoys," Wimarc said. "No telling what they found down there. Whatever it was, they weren't ready for it. Any specifics?"

"Just the standard default warning with a verbal addendum," Savaric said. "Something about 'white death.'"

Unlike his prior envoys, Wimarc had no affiliation with the corporate military. The corporate security forces garrisoned on Gunnora protected coalition property, smothered uprisings in the fringe territories, and kept general order through tyrannical martial law. A formidable fighting force, their brawn far surpassed their tactical understanding and overall intelligence. In an intense firefight against a heavily armed foe, the coalition's militia almost always had the upper hand.

In a delicate catch-and-cruise mission like the one lined up for them on Celestria, the ineptitude of the security force resulted in calamity, particularly when faced with an invisible enemy.

Wimarc and the other Myrmidons had the benefit of first-rate military training coupled with hands-on experience. They had worked all the dirty jobs too insignificant for the heavy-handedness of the security forces, from hunting pirates preying on merchant ships to rounding up blockade runners supplying rebels. Part mercenary, part police officer, part enforcer, Wimarc had earned a reputation in the field for getting the job done quickly, quietly, and with a minimum of firepower.

Approximately 10,000 colonists had settled on Celestria, known in bureaucratic circles as FTC01266, most playing an active role in the mining operations or living a primarily agrarian lifestyle while transforming the landscape within an ever-expanding worldhouse. The paraterraforming of Celestria had already converted nearly 18 percent of the planet's surface into a habitable expanse. Outside the enclosure, Celestria's heavily cratered surface boasted bright frost deposits and dark plains comprised of cryovolcanic residue—not hostile, but certainly an uninviting environment.

While the water ice, carbon dioxide, silicates, and organic compounds detected spectrally had all been corroborated when the settlement was no more than an unoccupied station, robonauts did not find the subsurface ocean predicted by analysts. A thin atmosphere consisting of carbon dioxide and molecular oxygen surrounded the planet.

"According to Savaric, areas are scattered around the central command complex still showing active life support." Wimarc strapped himself and his team into the landing shuttle. "No confirmation on life signs at this point."

"What do you think is down there, chief?" Forwin had heard plenty of chatter back on Gunnora. He had run across freighter pilots and starfighters of the Frontier Detachment in the dodgy watering holes around the shipyards. They spoke of strange incidents along the outer edges of coalition territory. Even veteran spacefarers shunned Celestria, maintaining that it should have been left uninhabited. "Some say it may have been an alien outpost long ago."

"And that alien ghosts took down an entire settlement and destroyed three Dione class cutters," Wimarc said, casting a glance over his shoulder. "I don't know exactly what to expect, but my gut tells me this is no different than what happened on Rhuddlan 100 years ago or on the ocean planet Gwenddwr." In both instances, the coalition-backed governorship had failed, leading to bloody civil wars that culminated in widespread systems failures and, ultimately, death for most of the colonists. "I think we'll find a handful of survivors hiding from the coalition because they know they'll be prosecuted."

"And if you're wrong?" Only Forwin, Wimarc's miraculous engineer and overworked mechanic, could chide the Myrmidons' leader without provoking a fistfight. Physically, he was broad-shouldered and thickset, and his muscles matched his technical prowess. "I mean, you are fallible, after all."

"Then I guess we're about to go for a stroll over some alien graves," Wimarc said, keying in the flight plan. In a few minutes they would be looking for a suitable landing site. "Let's hope we don't annoy any of them."

2.

"Another salvage effort has arrived." Cyberneticist Matityahu Holman studied the configuration of the vessel that had just entered orbit over Celestria. He spoke to no one in particular since he found himself alone in Mission Control, sitting at an otherwise unmanned row of instrument panels. The station's primary computer identified the visiting spacecraft and reported its findings. "Interesting," Holman said, surprised that his guests did not appear to have official clearance from the First Trade Coalition. "Scavengers, already?"

The computer—consistently suspicious—urged defensive action and awaited further instruction.

"You are too distrustful," Holman said. "I'll have no part in initiating any more violence. These hands have enough blood on them already."

He wished he could circumvent the failsafe protocol that went into effect when the crisis struck Celestria. He wished he could find a way to sidestep the communication blackout, respond to the ship's hails, and transmit a warning, an explanation, or a plea for help. Holman lacked the security clearance required to force the colony's systems to stand down.

"Like those who came before, they're here to liberate the survivors," Holman said, his tone bitter. All previous rescue attempts had failed miserably—and he had been utterly powerless, forced to watch rescuers perish. "I may not be able to help them, but I most won't hinder them."

The cyberneticist vacated an ergonomically snug chair and paced through aisles of empty workstations, some still adorned with the personal effects of Mission Control personnel who had succumbed to the White Death. Prior to the epidemic, he had only set foot in the settlement's hub once, during his orientation. For the past year, however, the nerve center and the adjoining chambers had become his home—and his dungeon.

Torment in this torture chamber came from seclusion, silence, and infinite hours of introspection and regret.

Holman had no fear of starvation since a lifetime's worth of provisions had been stored within the enclosure. Though lacking in epicurean delights, the stores included palatable food and an ample supply of water.

Outside the fortified walls of the central command complex's castellated nucleus, beyond the blast doors and the improvised reinforcement network Holman had hastily constructed as the scourge swept through the worldhouse, the product of the apocalyptic pestilence haunted the ruins of the colony.

3.

Following an uneventful descent, landing shuttle *Madeline* from the frigate *Rattlesnake* put down on the surface of Celestria, an icy planetoid orbiting a red dwarf star found along the outermost edges of space claimed by the First Trade Coalition of Earth. On board, Wimarc Essex and three members of his Myrmidons—all sporting cutting-edge, armored, skintight counterpressure spacesuits—prepared to look for survivors of the colony.

Coming to rest just outside the worldhouse on a relatively smooth, bright plain punctuated by knobs and pits, Wimarc realized that two of the colony's enclosure panels had been forcibly dislodged from the inside of the structure. Visuals also revealed another surprise: The patchy white substance covering the surface of Celestria was not ice.

"You see that, don't you?" Wimarc squinted, trying to comprehend the images cycling across a pair of compact view screens on his control panel. The pictures came from ventral cams mounted near the landing struts. "Increase magnification by a factor of ten."

The enhanced picture showed densely packed clusters of cottony blobs crowned with white, leaf-like lobes.

"It looks like a fungus," Aldred said. "But, how can it survive in this atmosphere?"

"Lichens can survive in space in a dormant state." Amiria doubled as the Myrmidons' medical and science officer. She had collected half a dozen degrees and certificates from various universities over the years—enough to settle down and launch a lucrative career in several fields. An adrenaline junkie, she preferred life in deep space, traversing the heavens on dicey missions. "Subject them to extreme temperatures, cosmic radiation, the vacuum of space—once they rehydrate, they're perfectly fine."

"Not that it should come as a surprise to anyone," Aldred said, "but onboard, short-range sensors confirm the enclosure has depressurized with a total loss of artificial atmosphere." He continued reading incoming data, picking and choosing pertinent information. "Two panels have been displaced through detonation."

"There are only two scenarios in which a colonial governor would give that order," Wimarc said, initiating a 10-second countdown before blowing the hatch. "It might be given as a last resort to put out an otherwise uncontrollable fire, preferably after isolating colonists in pressurized safe cells." He paused, turned, and faced the others. "I see no evidence of a firestorm."

"Then, what's the other scenario?" Forwin asked, his sarcasm palpable. "I mean, as if I didn't already know."

"Invasion," Wimarc answered. "Potentially by an alien life form."

"There's something else, chief." Even as the cabin depressurized and the gangplank extended to the planet's surface, Aldred reviewed the last bits of new data. "Before they detonated the worldhouse shielding, there are signs it had already been breached. It looks like there are hundreds, thousands maybe, of micro-fissures. Defects, maybe. Hard to tell. All of them would have been automatically sealed, though."

Crossing the dreary basin to reach the closest access gate in the enclosure, the four found an unfamiliar and unsettling arrangement of stars pinned to the black veil overhead. The ruins of the worldhouse, lacking any striking signs of devastation and catastrophe, nonetheless magnified the oppressive gloom of the apathetic twilit skies and the desolation of the unconquered Celestrian landscape. Before them stood the bleak, sterile walls that once embraced and safeguarded the colonists' lives.

These same walls likely sheltered none but the dead now.

Those minute fungi blanketed the ground and coated the exterior of the enclosure to an average height of 20 meters. Wimarc felt his boots crush the crystal-like life forms with each footfall and watched as a sinister cloud formed in their wake as they progressed across the landscape. Wimarc noticed, too, as they advanced, the tiny, flaky, alabaster things began to undulate rhythmically, their crusty ridges rippling softly.

Since none of the others noticed the phenomenon, he kept the revelation to himself.

Inside the worldhouse, more appalling scenes of destruction and deterioration awaited. Therein, illuminated by the diffuse glow of slowly dimming artificial lighting, the doom that came to the Celestria settlement abundantly itself in the frozen corpses of ill-fated colonists. Some died alone, unable to reach the safety of a pressurized cell. Some died hand-in-hand or locked in an embrace with a spouse, a lover, or a stranger who shared a fear of meeting death unaccompanied.

The team also found bodies piled deep near certain portals leading to safe cells, the remains of residents who found themselves trapped outside when the panels had been dislodged. Desperate for shelter, but denied sanctuary by those inside, they expired as the artificial atmosphere ebbed.

All of the dead shared one significant attribute: Each one had been encased in a gauzy veil of white fungi.

From their point of entry, Wimarc and his team hiked three kilometers to the colony's central district. The unsymmetrical worldhouse had fanned out over thousands of square hectares during the settlement's first two centuries, expanding in certain quarters to encompass the prime pieces of Celestrian real estate. Several mining stations had been established, and much of the land area had been converted for agricultural use, sustaining the population.

At the core of the colony rested a once-thriving city, Kymric, its twisting, narrow cobbled lanes and dark gray towers evoking a form of structural design more suitable to medieval Europe. Quarried and cut using high-tech precision lasers, the raw materials came from the surrounding environment. The available rock strongly resembled Purbeck Marble, a blue-gray sedimentary limestone long ago utilized in the construction of English cathedrals, possibly inspiring Celestria's city planners to adopt a Neo-Gothic style in developing the city.

Kymric featured soaring structures and lavish alcazars, now all silent and still. Its most impressive edifices emphasized verticality and light, employing ribbed vaults and flying buttresses. Between each building's narrow buttresses, large, ornate windows captured and magnified the scarlet hues of the local red dwarf star.

The niveous, fleecy fungi possessed perpetual mandate over all within the worldhouse, overspreading each building with a snow-white sheath and cloaking each corpse with a hoary shroud. Kymric had become an eerie, tricolor world, painted by chalky whites, ashen grays, and dull, sanguine reds.

At the heart of the city, Wimarc and his team found the central command complex. Light poured through the grand doors of the main entrance, sheltered by a pillared portico. Several more colonists had died here, ascending the stairs, their pasty corpses petrified into frantic poses of apparent torment, preserving their final moments of life.

Through their visors, the team members peered across a wide atrium and down the long corridor leading deep into the facility. Two figures, their features concealed by the omnipresent fungi, slumped forward in their chairs, frozen behind the center's reception desk. Though the section of the building had not lost interior lighting, the automatic doors had never sealed, and the life support systems had not been activated.

"Beyond that first blast door 150 meters down the hall," Aldred said, "life support is functioning properly."

"I can't get a clean reading on life signs," Amiria said. "There's too much background noise. Might be the fungi interfering with the scanners."

"We need to get in there," Wimarc said, gesturing toward the far end of the corridor. "Amiria, take Forwin and see if you can bypass security and get us through the blast door. Aldred," Wimarc scraped a patch of white fungus off the desktop and placed a small wireless keypunch on the surface along with a selection of colored cables. "I still want access to their security systems. Let's try a manual connection."

"Not necessary, chief," Aldred said. "Something—someone—unlocked the system. I have full access to the surveillance cams now on my handheld."

"How about the colony's main database?" Wimarc started scanning the available files using his own compact viewer. "Can you find journal entries, encoded messages that were never transmitted—anything that might explain what happened?"

"Negative. All I have is cam access. Like someone wanted us to see something."

As the system ran through a seemingly endless sequence of surveillance cameras, Wimarc and Aldred scrutinized each image. The pictures captured the lost colony's many ghostlike vistas and underscored the disquieting tranquility and ghastly hush that had displaced the once lively, flourishing community. From shadowed alcoves along the streets of Kymric to the sprawling fields of withered crops swathed in albescence, the bleak, lonely scenery of Celestria evoked phantom fears long dismissed by science and conjured thoughts of ancient superstitions.

"Wait," Wimarc leaned closer to the monitor. "Pause on that one," but before Aldred could react, the image vanished. The screen showed the front steps leading up to the main entrance of the central command complex. "Keep watching," Wimarc said, walking toward the double doors. "I'll be right back."

Standing at the top of the steps beneath the pillared portico, Wimarc studied the bodies scattered before him. He counted 16 corpses now—though, on the way in, he only recalled seeing 11. He knelt, watching the one closest to him for more than a minute—observing his extremities, examining the fungi encasing him in detail.

When he was convinced, he stood and went back into the central command complex.

"They've moved," Wimarc said, returning to the reception desk. His customary composed demeanor remained intact, though his eyes betrayed an embryonic apprehension that unnerved Aldred. "They're not dead—they're climbing the stairs out there."

"Chief," Amiria's voice sounded choppy and hesitant through the communication device. "You need to get down here. The bodies down here—most of them were hit with blasters before this place lost atmosphere. This was a real massacre, easily 15 to 20 casualties ..."

"Listen," Forwin interrupted Amiria, addressing Wimarc directly. "If you can get the door on that end of the hallway to seal, I can activate life support in this section."

Wimarc and Aldred entered the corridor and used an emergency control located behind an access panel to seal the door. As they sprinted down the corridor to meet Amiria and Forwin, breathable air filled the compartment as both pressure and some degree of warmth returned. The fungi blanketing the floor and covering the walls reacted to the change in atmosphere conditions almost immediately: Each entity rippled with newfound life, its crystalline structure softening as it distended itself as if awakening from an extended period of hibernation.

Alarmingly, the fungi on the floor parted as Wimarc and Aldred advanced, presenting them with a clear path.

"Get the blast door open," Wimarc called as he and Aldred approached their companions. He anticipated what would happen next and realized they had very little time. "Get it open now!"

Many of the bodies Amiria had reported had already begun to stir with an aberrant, perverted form of vigor. Clearly no longer living, the corpses of the colonists displayed an appalling mode of animation fueled by the fungi enfolding them. As Wimarc arrived on the scene, he noticed that more than half had been rendered useless as hosts through violent decapitation.

"Aim for their heads," the leader of the Myrmidons commanded as the dead colonists took to their feet.

4.

Sequestered in the mission control room of the central command complex, cyberneticist Matityahu Holman monitored the determined progress of four would-be rescuers, sent to Celestria to recover or recoup whatever remained. He had watched as they slogged across the barren achromatic fields, a white haze suspended just above the ground inscribing their progress. He had disabled the weapon systems to allow them safe passage and had managed to unlock security access to provide them access to the surveillance cams. Still, he feared even with his assistance they would not manage to reach his inner sanctum.

The White Death, long quiescent in the chill of Celestria's natural atmosphere, had detected the intrusion. After months of contemplative slumber, it stirred to life once more. Through the surveillance cameras, Holman watched as the confrontation in the corridor took shape—watched as long-dead colonists—now hosts to the dreadful, parasitic scourge—coordinated their attack.

Still, none of the other teams had made it as far as this group. Holman hoped the liberators would not underestimate the entities.

"It's happening again," Olluna said, eying the monitors. "Must we watch another massacre?"

"You don't have to watch if you don't want to."

Holman's niece Olluna drifted through the chamber. The young woman—infinitely more perceptive than her uncle—had arrived at Celestria only hours before fate or the ineptitude of science brought calamity to the colony. Studious and insightful, she had easily unraveled the mystery of the outbreak, though Holman would not willingly substantiate her theory. His acknowledgment of guilt, though, could be found in the hours he spent in seclusion, reflecting on his hubris and his culpability.

"They aren't like the others, are they?" She watched as Wimarc and his Myrmidons faced carriers of the White Death. "Maybe we'll finally get away from this place."

"Don't get your hopes up," Holman said. "You know as well as I do that those things won't give up easily. There are more assembling in the atrium, moving much more quickly now. They've been stockpiling energy, biding time."

"They're trying to open the door," Olluna said. The portal between the atrium and the corridor fell outside Holman's improvised defense network, augmented by Olluna's resourcefulness. Given sufficient time, the things would be able to access the security code and unlock the doorway. "They'll lose life support in the corridor."

"More importantly, when it depressurizes, they'll probably be swept back out into Kymric, right into the clutches of those things."

"You have to do something." Olluna, sprightly and graceful, weaved through the aisles until she located the right control panel. Since the last rescue attempt had failed, she had familiarized herself with mission control and had formulated several strategies. "See, I can force the door to re-sequence its access code every 45 seconds."

"That will slow them down some," Holman admitted. "It won't stop them, though. When they work together as a collective, they can process information faster than the mainframe."

"Then we'll have to put up more obstacles to keep them occupied, won't we?"

5.

Wimarc and his Myrmidons, their backs to a blast door in the central command complex on Celestria, faced eight reanimated corpses roused from near dormancy by the sudden rush of atmosphere in the contained chamber.

"Remember, these things aren't human anymore," Wimarc said. The chief of the Myrmidons had deduced that the all-pervading, alabaster fungi somehow controlled these dead bodies; and that the "White Death," as the quarantine beacon had called it, had wiped out to the Celestrian settlement.

While Wimarc had great respect for the dead, he had to protect his crew.

The first plasma bursts from Amiria's blaster ruptured the torso of one of the things, spinning him around on his feet and ripping his right arm from its socket. Still, the corpse shambled forward once it had regained its equilibrium, spilling its crusty entrails as it continued its attack.

The second volley wrenched its bobbing skull from its shoulders, sending it flying back down the hallway several meters. The decapitated body tumbled to the floor.

"Take off their heads." Wimarc repeated his instructions, demonstrating on a second corpse. His shot disintegrated the corpse's skull and dissolved his putrid brain.

A few moments later, the corpses had all been beheaded and Forwin and Aldred were busy roasting the fungi in the hallway.

"Have you ever seen anything like this?" Wimarc continued working on opening the blast door, hoping that on the other side, he would find only survivors. "I came here expecting rebels—maybe aliens. I didn't plan on zombies."

"If you are asking for a scientific explanation," Amiria said, "I can offer you several examples in nature of parasitic forms of life taking over the dead bodies of plants and animals. I've never seen anything capable of hijacking a human, though."

"This damn thing has been completely rewired from the inside." Wimarc's growing frustration went unnoticed by his science officer. "Someone must have survived in there," he said. "It would be nice if they'd let us in before a mob of these things comes shuffling into the hallway."

Amiria knelt, hovering over a nearby corpse. Most of the fungi had been blackened, though several small spots remained unscathed. As she watched, the white patches expanded as the surviving entities resurrected the charred fungi. Instinctively, she knew the speed of the process all but ruled out any kind of natural biological function. Using a handheld scanner, she examined the entities in minute detail, studying them at a molecular level.

"I knew it," Amiria said, her conceit mixed with a trace of panic. She stood, lurching backward, trying to put some distance between her and the corpse. "It's not a fungus," she said. "They're mechanical, at least in part. Nanobots. Don't touch them."

"'Don't touch them?'" Wimarc shot her a cynical glance, then looked toward the floor. She followed his gaze down to his boots. Nanobots coated his spacesuit from the tips of his feet to just below his knees. She found a similar dispersion over her own suit. "I suppose you're going to tell me they're going to try to get inside the suit, too."

Amiria started to respond but found her communication device dead.

Forwin and Aldred had swept the entire corridor, their blasters cooking the entities as they went. Returning, they found vast new swathes of white, leaf-like lobes spreading from the floor to the ceiling, undulating as they passed. The things multiplied at a dizzying rate, threatening to close in around them and engulf them. They tried to blast their way back down the hall, but soon found themselves completely surrounded. Back to back, they could keep the things at bay but could not proceed any further without risking direct contact.

"I need options now," Wimarc said, mouthing the words slowly so Amiria could understand. Both of them had lost communications now. Tapping his weapon, he added, "Blasters won't get us out of this."

"Thinking, chief," she nodded. She took a few tentative steps forward to see how the nanobots would react. As she advanced, she noticed her handheld scanner flashed to life, its display scrolling through the startup menu. Moving back a single step, the scanner went blank. She gestured to Wimarc, instructing him to stand in a specific spot. "There's some kind of dampening field, here," she said. "That's why our com went out. It stretches out from the blast door about two meters."

"Someone must have just activated it. That's a start," Wimarc said. "Doesn't help Forwin and Aldred at the moment, though." He could no longer see the other Myrmidons, though he could still see flashes from their blasters. The cottony nanobots had encircled them. "How do we get them here?"

"Already on it." Amiria did not waste time explaining that she could rig the scanner to set off an electromagnetic pulse that would momentarily inhibit the nanobots. Generating the local EMP would, however, render the apparatus useless. As she leaned forward to remove the scanner from the effects of the dampening field, the clever nanobots began erecting a wall, stacking themselves in an attempt to reach the device. "They won't have much time to get down here," she said, completing the modification. "We only get one shot. Here we go."

Wimarc heard a sharp crack through his communication link, followed by absolute silence. Lights in the corridor flickered and failed, replaced by faint secondary lighting. The nanobots did not move.

Forwin and Aldred burst through the white curtain and bolted down the corridor, crushing everything in their path.

Wimarc looked at Amiria, hoping she could tell him how long they had before the nanobots would reactivate—hoping she had another idea. She shrugged, dropping the damaged scanner to the floor.

Just as Forwin and Aldred arrived at the end of the corridor, the nanobots awoke from their short nap, aggravated. They constructed a solid wall just outside of the dampening field.

"They're biding their time now," Wilmarc said. He guessed that dozens, possibly hundreds of nanobot-infested colonists had gathered in the atrium. They would be working to get through the doorway on the opposite end of the corridor. When it opened, they would all be swept outside. "We could use a miracle about now."

At that instant, the blast door opened. On the other side, a young woman stood smiling.

"Welcome to Celestria," Olluna said. "I will have to ask you to remove your spacesuits."

6.

Wimarc, Amiria, Forwin, and Aldred sat around a long oval meeting table in what once served as a formal conference room for visiting dignitaries. After a somewhat embarrassing exchange in the corridor in which everyone had been asked to fully disrobe—with swarming nanobots scrambling just outside the dampening field—ginger-haired Olluna had provided each of the Myrmidons with suitable articles of clothing. She had remained detached until a set of rigorous scans had confirmed that none of the visitors had picked up a minuscule hitchhiker outside the central command complex.

"Your shuttlecraft has been compromised." Olluna, assuming the role of convivial hostess, set a pitcher of Gunnoran Stout on the faux mahogany tabletop. Six frosted mugs had already been placed on crystal coasters scattered around the table. "Please, help yourselves."

After she keyed in an access code in a wall panel, a concealed monitor materialized. It displayed an image of the *Madeline,* its hull caked with throngs of alabaster nanobots. "They're dismantling it for parts," Olluna reported, her voice remarkably composed for someone whose chance at freedom appeared to be coming apart at the seams. "They'll strip the vessel within a few hours, even under the harsh conditions. They did the same thing with the three cutters that landed."

"And the rescue teams?" Wimarc filled his mug. "What happened to them?"

"Ambushed in Kymric." Keying in another sequence of numbers, Olluna showed crowds of dead colonists, their bodies commandeered by the White Death, as they congregated in the cobbled streets outside the complex. The hideous scenes seemed conjured from dark industrial-age nightmares and exposed in shuffling madness the gruesome consequence of technology uninhibited by moral codes. "They spent too much time out there. Their suits couldn't protect them," she said. "Neither could yours, you know. Another few minutes and you would have been infected."

"Where did those things come from?" Amiria turned away from the monitor, unable to stomach the horror any longer. "That technology has been banned for centuries."

"Laws are open to interpretation in the fringe territories." Matityahu Holman entered the room, his emaciated form and pallid expression suggesting he had been depriving himself of adequate food and rest. After formally introducing himself and his niece, he returned to Amiria's question. "Celestria was no ordinary colony," he explained. "It was a testing ground for the First Trade Coalition."

"A testing ground for what?" Wimarc sipped the bitter stout ale. His thoughts turned to Idonea Haversham, the regional supervisor, who had sent him on this fool's errand. He found himself wondering if she had known about the scourge of Celestria all along.

"As the coalition's chief cyberneticist, I was asked to augment all of the colonists with brain implants and other forms of cyberware and nanodevices, with or without their permission. The implants would enhance strength, sensory perception, memory, and cognitive ability." Holman could sense Wimarc's growing distrust. "The coalition was determined to test these breakthroughs in nanotechnology. I warned them that it was too soon."

"Yet here you are," Wimarc said. "What went wrong?"

"For the first 20 years, nothing went wrong," Holman said defensively. He had overseen thousands of procedures since his arrival and devoted decades to perfecting the science. He had cultivated a flawless cybernetic improvement regimen, a regime set in motion practically from birth. "I introduced various biotech implants designed to compensate for abrupt changes in the environment—previously a stumbling block for space exploration, thanks to our species' rather sluggish capacity to adapt on a Darwinian evolution scale.

"But, a little over one Terran year ago, the nanobots evolved unexpectedly." Holman's gaze strayed, his eyes fixing on the awful, shambling White Death that filled the streets of Kymric. "They underwent a sweeping, comprehensive metamorphosis, becoming composite organisms—a symbiotic pairing of a nanomite and an organic photobiont harvested from human genetic material."

"You almost make it sound poetic," Wimarc said. "You overlook the fact that their genesis came at the expense of their host humans."

"Trust me, Captain—not a day goes by that I don't calculate my shame and search for ways to express my grief."

"You're saying they're miniature cybernetic organisms." Amiria did not try to hide either her skepticism or her admiration. "You have created something that is part machine and part animal, a new life form."

"One that is unfriendly," Forwin added. "I don't care what they are at this point. I want to know how to kill them so we can get off of this rock."

"Your ship," Holman said, turning to Wimarc. "It is a Callisto class frigate, isn't it?"

"Yes," Wimarc answered. "The *Rattlesnake*."

"Then you should have a second landing shuttlecraft aboard," Holman continued. "There's a small landing pad above this complex. It was used as a terminus for small hovercars inside the worldhouse, but it will accommodate one of your shuttles."

"What about the nanobots?" Wimarc knew the exterior of the complex had been covered. "What will stop them from contaminating the ship's hull while we're boarding?"

"Olluna has discovered a way to shift the dampening bubble we created." Holman patted his niece on the shoulder to show his pride in her ingenuity. Her fortuitous arrival at the onset of his most demanding tribulation had been a blessing; without her, he doubted his defense network would have been capable of holding off the horde. "She will program a path so that we can rendezvous with the shuttlecraft."

"Only one problem," Wimarc said. "Our com system isn't powerful enough to penetrate the complex." He glanced at Aldred, who nodded in agreement. "We'll have to wait to signal the shuttlecraft when we're topside. It'll take a good 30 minutes to get that ship down here."

"I can't guarantee that the dampening field will maintain its integrity for that length of time." Olluna paused, assessing her calculations. "There are too many variables to predict an outcome. Repositioning the field to cover the exterior of the complex may overload the circuits. It may cause the system to default, or it may terminate it completely."

"In that event," Forwin said, "we're back to throwing stones at the zombies."

7.

Matityahu Holman waited in Mission Control, surveying the relics of lost lives. He studied digital snap videos, which would continue to play long after humanity had forgotten about Celestria. He prodded smooth stones plucked from mountain streams on Earth, carried to the farthest reaches of coalition territory. He examined a collection of beer bottle caps collected from breweries scattered over hundreds of star systems.

Holman knew he had to admit his failings to the coalition. He had gone one step too far, tried to push the technology beyond its natural limits. He had encouraged the symbiotic relationship between the nanobots and their hosts, knowing the risks. He felt the benefits far outweighed the hazards—that death, even on a massive scale, could be justified if the product exceeded the value of the sacrifice.

"Everything is ready, sir." Olluna intruded on his musings. "Wimarc has asked that we suit up."

"I've told you a thousand times," Holman said. "You can call me uncle."

"It would be a counterfeit designation. I appreciate your kindness and consideration in circumventing my protocols. Allowing me to fulfill my mission would have been a more logical course of action, though."

"An unnecessary one, though."

"That remains to be seen."

8.

The Myrmidons took up defensive positions around the perimeter of the landing pad, outfitted in pressurized spacesuits that lacked both the armor and the comfort of the ones they had to abandon due to contamination.

Carrying plasma drills that made clumsy but efficient weapons, they had successfully cleared the pad of nanobots using the tools' weakest setting. Olluna's dampening bubble hovered just beneath the platform, acting as an impassible barrier.

From their vantage point, they could see much of the ruins of Kymric. At first glance, it seemed like an old Earth city blanketed in a light dusting of snow. The vast dome of the worldhouse spread overhead, towering columns supporting its bulk. From here, the Celestria colony retained a hint of its former majesty and beauty.

Closer inspection revealed the sallow phantasmagoria that had supplanted the colony. Wimarc watched Holman as he stood near the edge of the landing pad, staring down into the chaos he had created. He felt the cyberneticist's anguish, but he also felt his reprehensible arrogance, a lingering smugness that refused to be stifled by the catastrophic repercussions of his work.

His grief, Wimarc knew, could never displace his vanity.

"This is Savaric." Wimarc turned his attention to the worldhouse shielding. "I'm approaching from the east. I can see the opening," he said. Aldred and Forwin had managed to detonate a cluster of four panels, providing direct access to the shuttlecraft. "I'll be on the ground in one minute, pending clearance."

"You're cleared," Wimarc said. "Get us the hell out of here."

Olluna joined her uncle, peering down into the city one last time. He put an arm around her, urging her to rest her head on his shoulder. She showed even less remorse than Holman, though Wimarc questioned her role in all this. He detected something aberrant in her behavior that led him to unsettling speculation. Her lack of fear troubled him the most.

"The damping field is fluctuating." Amiria double-checked the scanning device Olluna had given her. "It's failing."

"Hold your positions," Wimarc said, charging the plasma drill. He switched over to the most powerful setting and ordered his crew to do the same. "We can still do this."

The first wave of nanobots surged over the rim of the landing pad. Holman staggered back several steps, nearly losing his balance. Olluna caught him, dragging him out of harm's way for the moment.

The bulky drills yielded much larger plasma bursts than standard-issue blasters. They lacked elaborate guidance systems and output consistency but packed a highly destructive punch. Forwin, the first Myrmidon to test the tool's effectiveness, vaporized all the nanobots in front of him. He also disintegrated a sizable chunk of the landing platform and blew a hole in a neighboring building.

Wimarc and Aldred fired simultaneously, causing the platform to shudder beneath them. Cracks appeared on the surface. Amiria fired next, the kickback knocking her off her feet. She recovered quickly.

"What's happening down there?" Savaric's voice betrayed his alarm. Wimarc had briefed him privately: He had warned him to abort the mission if he felt it necessary. "Am I still cleared for landing?"

"Blow the hatch on the way in," Wimarc said. "Catch-and-cruise, no time for civilities."

"Understood."

As Savaric approached, the flashes of plasma accelerated. He could see the White Death clambering over the exterior of the complex, the throngs of reanimated corpses filling the streets. The frayed and crumbling edges of the landing pad receded with each shot fired.

"Wimarc," Savaric said, yelling into the com. "Keep that up, and I won't be able to land!"

"If we stop firing, we're dead." Wimarc looked up at the shuttlecraft. As he had ordered, the hatch had been opened. "Don't touch down," he said. "Get as close as you can."

As the shuttle descended, more than a dozen corpses poured through the portal onto the airbridge connecting the complex with the landing pad. They lurched forward, moving more swiftly than before. Forwin spun on his heels, blasting the four leaders into nothingness. Two others lost an arm and a leg each and a third ended up in a pile of frothy, pasty ooze that had once been his torso.

Before Forwin could fire again, two others tackled him.

"Get them off!" The corpses, controlled by the White Death, mauled him viciously, tearing at his spacesuit and biting him with mechanically enhanced strength. "Wimarc!"

In an instant, Forwin's visor had shattered, and his suit had been breached. The nanobots poured through the slender cracks, invading the spacesuit and inserting themselves into Forwin's body through every accessible orifice.

Aldred fired the shot that incinerated him.

"It's no use," Olluna said, pulling away from Holman. "I have a responsibility to put an end to this."

"No, we're going to make it this time," Holman said. "We'll get away from here. You don't have to do anything."

"The coalition expects me to do my job," Olluna said. "Just like they expected you to do yours. You should know—you engineered me as the antidote in the event anything ever went wrong."

"It's not fair," Holman said. "You're my only family."

"I'm not family. I'm a facsimile of a relative you lost years ago."

Olluna began disassembling herself, disengaging the billions of nanobots that so precisely presented the likeness of Holman's niece. Holman wept, more devastated at the loss of his creation than he had been by the unintentional genocide he had authored on Celestria.

"You must tell them," Olluna said, looking up into his eyes as she continued her dissolution. "Tell them what happened here, uncle."

As the nanobots that comprised Olluna dispersed, they took on the crimson color that had been Olluna's ginger hair. They scattered quickly, advancing in all directions until they encountered the aggressive White Death.

The red nanobots speedily assimilated the white ones, deactivating them as they multiplied. Scarlet streamers spread across the building's exterior, washed through the streets of Kymric and well beyond, stretching to the far ends of the worldhouse and the barren, undeveloped lands beyond its protective shields.

"It's time to go, Holman," Wimarc said, holding out a hand. The shuttlecraft hovered overhead. "You have a lot of explaining to do."

The old man looked up at the leader of the Myrmidons, then back to the spot on the landing pad where Olluna had last stood.

"'And darkness and decay,'" Holman said, quoting a line from a memorable tale written many millennia ago, "'and the Red Death held illimitable dominion over all.'"

The End

The Scent of Mothballs by Lee Clark Zumpe

I am the scent of mothballs,
the shadows at the back of
the drawer where little things
accumulate

I am bagged and boxed,
swathed in protective
plastic covers, pressed
in albums

I am relics and hand-me-downs,
heirlooms destined for pawn
shops in the hands of distant
generations

I am pieces of you forgotten,
packed into attic trunks,
visited by silverfish and
cockroaches.

The Somme by Lee Clark Zumpe

France, 1916

By day, dirt and sky
are inseparable gray ghosts,
and mist crawls across the blistered earth
like shambling death.

Corpses cower in muddy trenches;
former friends detached –
we are too timid to dig graves
beneath the artillery.

The wounded bleed silently
without hope of reprieve,
rotting beside us until
they fade to bone.

By night, the indifferent twilight
applies its provisional shroud
to the ruins of humanity
strewn across poisoned fields.

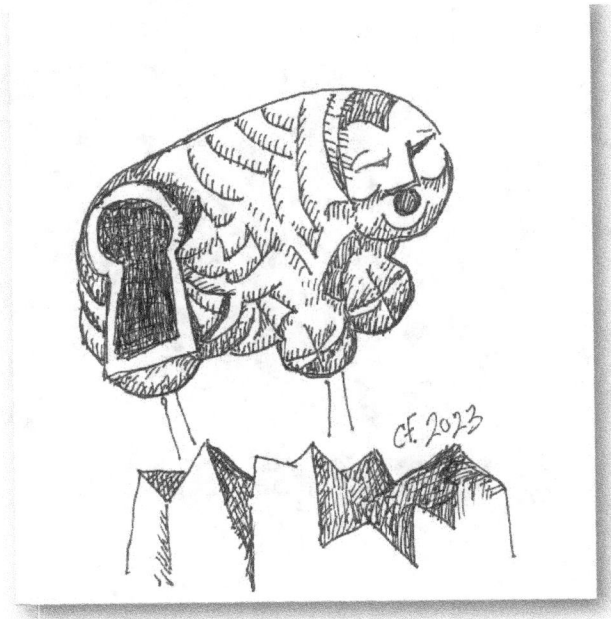

Night Gallery Movie Reviews

Haunted Mansion
Review by Lee Clark Zumpe

Disney conjures up a bewitching, E ticket-worthy "Haunted Mansion."

My childhood memories of Walt Disney World are inexplicably hazy. Between Oct. 1, 1971, the day Walt Disney World Magic Kingdom officially opened, and Grad Nite on May 17, 1986, I probably only visited the park on three or four occasions. I know my parents took me there once when I was still very young, within the first few years the park opened, because I recall unused ride coupons from the "value books" Disney sold at the main gate in the 1970s.

Other than the obligatory Grad Nite photograph, I have no snapshots to authenticate those visits. The only piece of memorabilia I have retained from that era is a Randotti skull, purchased from the Main Street Magic Shop.

Don't worry: I have enough Disneyana to fill several storage units today. I've acquired those collectibles throughout my adult life. And, throughout my adult life, I have made up for lost time at Walt Disney World. I have no idea how many times I've made the trek across I-4 to visit that Shangri-La of misplaced childhood, but it's probably well over 100 by now.

The Haunted Mansion was an opening day attraction at Magic Kingdom. As a kid who spent Saturday afternoons watching horrible old movies on *Creature Feature* and reading *Famous Monsters of Filmland*, Disney's dark ride attraction was—and continues to be—a must-do for me on every visit. From the stretching art gallery where guests are momentarily trapped by the Ghost Host to riding Doom Buggies through a labyrinthine haunted house carefully crafted by Imagineers, the entire experience is a fun, macabre excursion into a gothic horror story populated by campy ghosts.

Due to the success of the Pirates of the Caribbean franchise, Disney has made several attempts to adapt its theme park rides into cinematic ventures. The Haunted Mansion ride seems like an obvious choice, but a 2003 effort, "The Haunted Mansion" starring Eddie Murphy, generated unfavorable reviews despite modest success at the box office. More recently, Disney+ produced "Muppets Haunted Mansion" for Halloween in 2021.

Now, the ghosts are back in a new adaptation. *Haunted Mansion*, directed by Justin Simien, was released on July 28, 2023, by Walt Disney Studios Motion Pictures.

The story revolves around Gabbie (Rosario Dawson) and her son Travis (Chase Dillon). The two purchase and move into Gracey Manor, an old Southern manse, which Gabbie hopes to convert into a successful bed and breakfast. They quickly discover the estate is infested with unhappy haunts. Unlike most films, their immediate reaction isn't to stick around and investigate. They flee.

Unfortunately, the ghosts of Gracey Manor are very persistent. Once someone enters the house, there is no turning back. The ghosts pursue them and force them to return.

Gradually, Gabbie assembles a ragtag team to help solve the mystery and rid the house of its troublesome ghosts so she and her son can get on with their lives. Ben Matthias (LaKeith Stanfield), a reluctant hero whose own life has been upended by a recent tragedy, emerges as the group's de facto leader. Ben is an astrophysicist turned New Orleans ghost tour guide. Using his scientific background, he has developed a special camera capable of capturing the images of ghosts. Ben is recruited by Father Kent (Owen Wilson), the group's purported spiritual leader and resident exorcist.

Others who become entangled in the mansion's web are Harriet (Tiffany Haddish), a psychic; and Bruce Davis (Danny DeVito), a college history professor.

The team also forms an alliance with the ghost of Madame Leota (Jamie Lee Curtis), a legendary medium who was trapped in a crystal ball hidden in the attic of the mansion. Together, they learn that the ghosts are being manipulated by the Hatbox Ghost (Jared Leto), an evil entity, who is intent on adding one more soul to his collection of spirits.

I'll admit it: *Haunted Mansion* caught me off guard. Simien, working from a screenplay by Katie Dippold, effectively captures and recreates a lot of the Imagineering magic that makes the theme park attraction such a beloved ride. The film isn't just about jump scares, though: A lot of effort goes into character development.

There is depth in the script, and the cast conveys it and expands upon it through their performances. Stanfield is outstanding as Ben works through his grief. Haddish transforms what could have been a stereotypical spiritualist into something much more genuine: Harriet is a persistent woman who silently questions her own competence. In many ways, Travis is the heart of the story, and Dillon steals more than one scene.

The worst that can be said of the film is that it could have trimmed 30 minutes from its 125-minute runtime, which could have eliminated pacing problems. There are moments when it's difficult to follow the action, and the film breaks its internal logic. The story still manages to maintain suspension of disbelief.

Haunted Mansion isn't the kind of film that will walk away with a Doom Buggy full of awards. It's probably not even the kind of film that will fare well at the box office. It's definitely not a franchise-starter. At the same time, it's not just cinematic fluff or forgettable fun. It will resonate with hardcore Disney fans, and younger viewers who are just discovering the genre of scary movies. *Haunted Mansion* utilizes the dark ride as a springboard, but develops a unique, freestanding narrative that enhances the overall experience. That's a neat trick.

A major component of Simien's success in expanding the borders of the story beyond the parameters set by the existing ride is the distinct setting.

"The setting is New Orleans, a town that is predominantly Black," Simien said in the film's production notes. "New Orleans was one of the first places in the country where Black and Indigenous people could live freely and build wealth. Though this proved short-lived in the 19th century, it created an environment of cultural exchange that gave birth to jazz among many other early American phenomena.

"Exploring the production design of the original ride, the absence of artifacts from any people of color is striking and frankly suggests an origin for the mansion that was likely not intended by Walt Disney. It also didn't feel accurate or modern. There are British monarchs, Roman leaders and even mummies wandering this mansion; surely there'd be people of color. In this iteration, William Gracey, the original owner of the mansion, is fashioned in this version after one of the many wealthy free Creoles of Color that lived in New Orleans in the 19th century. Victor Geist, the organist, became a nod to Fats Waller. The waltzers are joined by lindy hoppers, can-can girls and other staples of Mardi Gras parades going back centuries."

Easily the most entertaining and imaginative adaptation of Disney's dark ride, *Haunted Mansion* is destined to be added to many family-friendly Halloween movie-viewing lists. It reverberates with all the creepy vibes of *The Addams Family, Beetlejuice, Little Shop of Horrors,* and *Ghostbusters,* but it doesn't mimic them. Its jump-scares are muted, and its antagonist is as menacing as any supernatural Disney villain. Filled with Easter eggs for Disney fans, *Haunted Mansion* is a satisfyingly spooky affair with a first-rate ensemble cast—and you probably won't have to stand in line to enjoy this ride.

Lee Clark Zumpe is entertainment editor at Tampa Bay Newspapers, a Tomatometer-Approved Critic, and an author of short fiction appearing in select anthologies and magazines. Follow Lee at www.patreon.com/Haunter_of_the_Bijou.

Renfield
Review by Lee Clark Zumpe

*Cartoonish carnage and explosive action make **Renfield** a guilty pleasure*

The man who introduced the world to the most unforgettable cinematic interpretation of the titular character from Bram Stoker's epistolary novel *Dracula* was born in 1880. Tod Browning directed and coproduced the 1931 Universal Pictures classic *Dracula*. Before that, Browning did something many of us have threatened to do at some point in our lives: He ran away and joined the circus.

At 16, Browning worked as a roustabout and a barker at sideshows, but eventually, he found his way to the stage as a contortionist. He concocted a live burial act billed as "The Living Hypnotic Corpse," he worked as a clown for Ringling Brothers, and he was a vaudeville performer—all this before making his directorial debut at 35 with the short silent film *The Lucky Transfer* in 1915.

Browning wrote and directed more than 50 films through 1939. He is primarily remembered for his horror titles, having earned the sobriquet "the Edgar Allan Poe of cinema" in the trade press. Of all his bizarre melodramas and horror mysteries, *Dracula* is the most universally recognized and discussed. The film has achieved its own immortality, as filmmakers and moviegoers alike acknowledge that Browning's version established many visual tropes that became touchstones for all vampire films—just as Stoker's novel instituted many of the conventions of Gothic vampire fiction.

Bela Lugosi portrayed Count Dracula in Browning's adaptation, creating an iconic and indelible visual archetype. For fans of the film, certain scenes are etched in memory: Dracula descending the staircase in his once stately castle, now neglected and deteriorating; the cloaked vampire standing menacingly above a sleeping young woman, leaning forward unhurriedly as he prepares to sink his fangs into her flesh; the moment Professor Van Helsing discovers Dracula has no reflection in the mirrored lid of John Harker's cigarette box.

And there's another equally enduring image from the 1931 *Dracula* that doesn't involve Lugosi. When the schooner *Vesta* arrives in England carrying Dracula's coffin, the crew is missing. As harbor workers search the vessel, they hear unnerving laughter which leads them to the ship's hold. There, staring up out of the darkness, is raving Renfield, a former solicitor who has become a zoophagous maniac as Dracula's custodial slave.

Renfield is played by Dwight Frye, an actor known for taking on neurotic, murderous characters. Frye's Renfield is as striking as Lugosi's Dracula.

Renfield is an integral part of Stoker's novel and has appeared in many cinematic adaptations since Frye's famous portrayal. Among the other actors who have played the part are Klaus Kinski, Arte Johnson, Tom Waits, Tony Haygarth, and Peter MacNicol.

Nicholas Hoult has joined the prestigious club of Renfield veterans. He plays the titular character in the horror-comedy *Renfield*, directed by Chris McKay. The film was released April 14, 2023, by Universal Pictures. Nicolas Cage stars as Dracula.

In modern day New Orleans, R.M. Renfield is well into his second century of thralldom as Dracula's concierge. He is a nurse, a caregiver, a guardian, a porter, a house-sitter, and a janitor. Mostly, though, he is an indentured servant, whose primary responsibility is providing his master with an endless procession of victims. In return for Renfield's loyalty, Dracula has bestowed upon him superhuman strength and agelessness—which he must activate and maintain by eating bugs.

Renfield has grown weary of his serfdom. He joins a support group where he listens to other people talk about their codependent relationships as he dreams of liberating himself from his narcissistic boss. In the meantime, he tries to justify his headhunting vocation by choosing abusive partners and other morally corrupt individuals to serve to Dracula for sustenance.

This strategy causes him to encounter members of New Orleans's reigning crime syndicate. Specifically, he crosses Teddy (Ben Schwartz), heir apparent of the Lobo crime family. Teddy's mother, Bellafrancesca (Shohreh Aghdashloo) is the current mob boss.

Renfield finds an unexpected ally in Rebecca Quincy (Awkwafina), a traffic cop who is eager to take down the seemingly untouchable Lobo operation and who senses corruption among law enforcement agents at the New Orleans Police Department. Renfield and Rebecca must work together as they attempt to defeat both the criminals and Dracula.

Renfield is by no means a masterpiece. There aren't any remarkable sequences that are likely to become engrained in pop culture. A hundred years from now, no one will be talking about the film's memorable tableaus, its arresting cinematography, or the outstanding performances of its cast. The plot is threadbare, and the humor is hit-or-miss.

And none of that really matters.

What *Renfield* delivers is sick, twisted fun. If you happen to be a fan of Lloyd Kaufman and Troma horror, or Charles Band and Full Moon Productions, "Renfield" is going to be right up your alley. Unlike the films from Troma and Full Moon, though, *Renfield* has an ample budget to make all the blood and guts convincingly ghastly—and a first-rate cast able to bring depth to cookie-cutter characters.

Give Cage vampire dental prosthetics, and you can rest assured he is going to gobble up the scenery. Cage is known for acting melodramatically in his films, and for gonzo performances that render his roles as over-the-top and exaggerated. In *Renfield*, that immoderation fits the role perfectly. His Dracula is simultaneously intimidating and absurd. He oozes with condescension and narcissism. Hoult paints a character that is hapless but repentant, obsessed with self-help books and determined to be a better person by exiting a toxic relationship.

The film's best performances come from Awkwafina and Aghdashloo. Even though the role of Rebecca deserved more lines, more development, and more screen time, Awkwafina conveys both her frustration and her fortitude. Aghdashloo's Bellafrancesca is as threatening an antagonist as any centuries-old vampire. It's fun to guess whether she will be Dracula's rival or ally as the plot progresses.

The centerpiece of the film is its explicit, shameless, ongoing splatterfest. *Renfield* features at least four extended fight sequences that are explosively violent and meticulously choreographed. Blood flows, limbs are torn from torsos, bodies explode, and innards dangle from gaping wounds. It's gruesome, horrific, and—unless you are squeamish—it's delightfully campy and wicked.

Renfield may not be a masterpiece, but it's more than disposable entertainment. It's a gratifying take on Stoker's creations, a quenching blend of excessive gore and cartoonish self-worship, and guilty pleasure for viewers who enjoy offbeat horror-comedy mashups.

Lee Clark Zumpe is entertainment editor at Tampa Bay Newspapers and an author of short fiction appearing in select anthologies and magazines. Follow Lee at www.patreon.com/Haunter_of_the_Bijou.

We Have a Ghost
Review by Lee Clark Zumpe

David Harbour tries to breathe life into Netflix flick **We Have a Ghost***.*

As I sit in the Tampa Bay Newspapers editorial office preparing to write this week's movie review, I am alone—probably. It's the weekend, and the building is empty, its cubicles currently untenanted. Monday morning, my coworkers will arrive, someone will fire up the Keurig, conversations will erupt spontaneously, and the weekly process of putting together newspapers will commence. For now, though, it is quiet, as it always is when I am alone in the office—except when it isn't.

Here's the thing: I don't really believe in ghosts. I watch paranormal shows, but I am a diehard skeptic. At the same time, I can't completely discount the possibility of ghosts. And this building, from time to time, likes to taunt me with seemingly inexplicable noises: footsteps crossing the laminate wood flooring in the reception area, doors opening and closing, chairs scraping the tile in the kitchen. Once, very early in the morning, a voice said "hello" as I made my way from the car to the front door. I replied before realizing I couldn't see anyone in the darkness.

I know that all these things can be explained without involving the so-called spirit world. I still allow myself the indulgence of thinking that it's possible we do occasionally encounter something inexplicable and uncanny.

Ghosts—the pretend variety—have been showing up in cinema since the late 19th century. In the 1896 French film *Le Manoir du diable*—released as "The Haunted Castle" in the United States—Mephistopheles conjures four specters to subdue a cavalier.

In the 1898 short film Photographing a Ghost, a group of documentarians attempt to take a picture of a ghost. The following year, Walter R. Booth directed The Miser's Doom, about a miner who is frightened to death by the ghost of someone he killed.

Cinematic ghosts can be scary, funny, dramatic, or romantic. They can be vengeful or playful, hostile or hospitable, bleak or beguiling. They can be Freddy Krueger, or they can be Casper the Friendly Ghost.

Director Christopher Landon's new film We Have a Ghost riffs on paranormal reality TV series and emulates common themes found in onscreen depictions of ghosts of the postmodern era. Released Feb. 4, 2023, on Netflix, the film struggles to engage viewers despite an appealing premise, some standout performances, and a mix of comedy, adventure, and mystery.

The film begins with the Presley family checking out a creepy old fixer-upper in a suburban Chicago neighborhood. The audience already knows it is haunted, but the Presleys—due to circumstances—are looking for something affordable. They purchase the property. It doesn't take long to discover the house comes with a ghost.

Kevin (Jahi Winston) finds the resident haunter while exploring the attic. The ghost (David Harbour)—who is found wearing a bowling league shirt with the name Ernest embroidered on the chest—attempts to frighten Kevin with classic ghostly antics. Recording the encounter with his phone, Kevin responds not with terror but with amusement. Soon, the two form a bond and Kevin offers to help the trapped soul remember his life and find out how he died.

Obstacles arise. First, Kevin's dad Frank (Anthony Mackie) sees the ghost as a cash cow. With the help of Kevin's older brother Fulton (Niles Fitch), Frank posts a series of videos featuring Ernest, which soon become a social media sensation. All the hype brings money, as well as throngs of supernatural groupies and story-hungry journalists that besiege the house.

As word of the ghost spreads, it attracts the attention of Dr. Leslie Monroe (Tig Notaro), a has-been paranormal researcher who alerts her former boss, Deputy CIA Director Arnold Schipley (Steve Coulter). Schipley—the kind of nefarious government agent that would fit right in with the Smoking Man from The X-Files—restarts a covert program designed to capture and enslave a ghost. He sends Monroe to apprehend Ernest.

Just from the synopsis, it's clear that We Have a Ghost isn't shy about borrowing elements—and in some instances entire scenes—from other movies. It's a mashup of tropes from Beetlejuice, Ghost, and E.T. the Extra-Terrestrial, among others. It directly references two of those films, either in the dialogue or with a visual cue.

The extent to which Landon evokes these films makes We Have a Ghost feel like a choppy pastiche rather than a clever parody. Frequent shifts in tone further undermine the coherence of the plot.

Harbour makes up for some of the film's shortcomings. In a nonspeaking role, he manages to breathe a lot of life into his unliving character. The audience senses his frustration, his isolation, his benevolence, and, as pieces of the puzzle start to fall into place, his courage and contentment.

Mackie and Winston make the best of what they're given. Landon's script doesn't dig deep enough into the father-son relationship to earn the viewer's empathy. There are clearly emotional cues that are supposed to resonate with the audience, but the lack of character development makes that investment difficult. That said, when Mackie does have an opportunity to connect in a heartfelt exchange with Kevin near the end of the film, he absolutely nails it.

In a film that seems to be inflated to excess with its runtime of just over two hours, many characters and story lines feel squandered. Isabella Russo, who stars as the Presley's neighbor Joy, should have had a bigger role—and could have, if the script hadn't glossed over the budding relationship between her and Kevin.

Notaro's character clearly had a backstory the audience never gets to see, so that when a change of conscience pushes her in different direction, it's unclear what motivates her.

Jennifer Coolidge also shows up to the party, playing popular TV medium Judy Romano. As always, Coolidge gets the laughs, but the scene feels like it was tacked on to provide a few madcap comic bits for the trailer.

We Have a Ghost is entertaining even if it fritters away most of its greatest aspects. A peripheral viewing may be the best approach: Expect scattered laughs, sentimentality, frantic action, and Amblin-esque charm, mixed with missed opportunities and underdeveloped and underutilized characters.

Lee Clark Zumpe is entertainment editor at Tampa Bay Newspapers and an author of short fiction appearing in select anthologies and magazines. Follow Lee at www.patreon.com/Haunter_of_the_Bijou.

Skinamarink

Review by Lee Clark Zumpe

*Arthouse horror **Skinamarink** relies on viewers to fill in the blanks.*

Have you ever had that dream where you walk around your house in the middle of the night, convinced you are awake, and suddenly realize something is amiss? You find an exterior door open, implying that some intruder entered while you slept. Furniture is missing or out of place. The floor plan of the house has been inexplicably altered, adding or deleting entire rooms. Family members are missing.

Panic escalates as you find yourself in an increasingly alien environment.

The book *Principles and Practice of Sleep Medicine* dedicates a chapter to idiopathic nightmares and dream disturbances associated with sleep/wake transitions.

Authors Tore Nielsen and Antonio Zadra describe false awakenings as being dream imagery in which the person is falsely waking up from sleep or from a dream, which leads to a state of "confusion while dreaming as to whether one is actually awake or asleep." Type 2 false awakenings are accompanied by a foreboding atmosphere and may include "hallucinations of ominous or anxiety-provoking sounds or strange apparitions of persons or monsters."

Been there, done that. I have also experienced sleep paralysis, a similar phenomenon that occurs between sleep and wakefulness. The accompanying hypnopompic hallucinations—involving the presence of a dangerous presence in the room—are as persuasive as they are terrifying.

The events depicted in *Skinamarink* appear to transpire within that murky borderland between the dream state and full, waking consciousness. *Skinamarink* is best described as an experimental horror film. It is the feature directorial debut of Kyle Edward Ball, who also wrote the screenplay. *Skinamarink* was released in select theaters on Jan. 13, 2023, through IFC Midnight. On Feb. 2, 2023, the film debuted on the horror streaming service Shudder.

The film's official synopsis explains: "Following a bizarre accident, a six-year-old girl and her four-year-old brother wake up one morning to discover all the doors and windows inside of their house have vanished. All the phones are dead, and the cable is out as well."

The children—Kevin (Lucas Paul) and Kaylee (Dali Rose Tetreault)—search the house for their father, but find they are alone. Their mother also is absent, and it is implied that she has not been present in the house for some time. Trying to cope with their situation, the children relocate to the living room where they watch old VHS tapes of cartoons on a television.

Doors and windows disappear. Strange and inexplicable sounds emanate from upstairs. Lights go on and off by themselves.

Skinamarink is set in 1995 and features an intentional lo-fi tone that showcases grainy, often indecipherable visuals, long takes, and an unnerving color palette. Some reviewers pigeonhole it as found footage horror, but that isn't compatible with the nature of the film's experimental format. Ball omits more than he reveals. In terms of the "show, don't tell" adage, he provides the bare minimum needed to establish narrative building blocks. There's nothing conventional about how the director conveys this unsettling, deliberately ambiguous story.

The viewer perceives their own subjective horror. Ball relies upon his audience to bring their own childhood trauma, their own abandonment issues, their own deep-seated fear and intense shame to the table.

"Skinamarink" is a twisted Rorschach test that will evoke different reactions from each person who accepts the challenge of sitting through the 100-minute run time. Its effectiveness is dependent upon the viewer's willingness to commune with certain core phobias and childhood memories of irrational — yet vivid — dread.

Because of the film's perplexing and often impenetrable dream logic, nothing depicted can be taken literally. Ball injects plenty of potential clues through eerie visuals, vague dialogue, and scattered bits of symbolism. Just when you think you have the mystery solved, though, something comes along and overturns your theory.

Skinamarink is an incomplete series of creepy sketches, and Ball asks the viewer to fill in the blank spaces with horrors plucked from their own imagination. Because it necessitates some level of viewer interface and because it obliges the audience to visit potentially uncomfortable memories or suppressed emotions, it is not for everyone. It is simultaneously tedious and terrifying. It is both provocative and frustrating.

For those willing to lose themselves in its atmospheric horror, *Skinamarink* is a surreal mix of high strangeness, acute anxiety and reflective melancholy. For others, it will likely come across as an overstretched, overindulgent art film that is more exasperating than frightening.

Ball made the film for a mere $15,000. According to Box Office Mojo, *Skinamarink* has grossed $1.9 million to date. That's a good sign that someone in Hollywood will want to see what Ball can do with a larger budget.

Lee Clark Zumpe is entertainment editor at Tampa Bay Newspapers and an author of short fiction appearing in select anthologies and magazines. Follow Lee at www.patreon.com/Haunter_of_the_Bijou.

The Pale Blue Eye

Review by Lee Clark Zumpe

*Harry Melling's depiction of Poe central to Netflix's **The Pale Blue Eye***

When someone mentions Edgar Allan Poe, most people will immediately recall the titles of some of his most famous works: *The Raven, The Tell-Tale Heart, The Cask of Amontillado*, and *The Fall of the House of Usher*. His name likewise evokes a certain image of a morbid author of macabre tales of Gothic horror revolving around themes of death, loss, anxiety, regret, and revenge. Though he may be remembered most for his horror stories, there is much more to be found in the works of Poe.

In addition to horror, Poe authored satirical pieces, humorous tales, and literary criticism. He contributed to the emerging genre of science fiction, influencing later authors such as Jules Verne and H.G. Wells. It may come as a surprise that Poe is widely considered to be the inventor of the detective fiction genre. He introduced the character C. Auguste Dupin, a professional detective, in 1841's *The Murders in the Rue Morgue*—arguably the first detective fiction story. Dupin returns to solve further crimes in Poe's stories, *The Mystery of Marie Rogêt* in 1842 and *The Purloined Letter* in 1844.

Did you know that before his writing career began in earnest, Poe enlisted in the United States Army? He served two years under an assumed name before being discharged in 1829. The same year, he accepted an appointment to the United States Military Academy at West Point, New York.

In *The Pale Blue Eye*, a new mystery thriller written and directed by Scott Cooper, a fictionalized version of Poe plays a pivotal role. The film was adapted from the 2003 novel of the same name by Louis Bayard. The film was released in select cinemas Dec. 23, 2022, before its streaming release on Jan. 6, 2023, by Netflix.

The Pale Blue Eye is set at West Point in 1830. Retired detective Augustus Landor (Christian Bale) is tapped to solve a grisly murder and mutilation at the military academy. A cadet has been found hanged. While his body lay in the academy's morgue, someone cut open the chest and removed the heart. Landor examines the corpse, discovering evidence overlooked by Dr. Daniel Marquis (Toby Jones), the West Point doctor who performed the autopsy.

Initially, Landor is met with a wall of silence. Most cadets are unwilling to share any practical information that can point the detective in the right direction. Of course, one cadet is eager to offer his opinion: Edgar Allan Poe (Harry Melling) giddily shares his theories with the stern and serious Landor. The detective is so impressed by his insight and his enthusiasm that he enlists his help in solving the case.

The Pale Blue Eye exhibits analogous elements found in recent 19th century police procedurals, and one can't help but compare it to British television series such as *Ripper Street* and *The Frankenstein Chronicles*, or the American series *The Alienist*. It leans heavily into its gothic stylings, employing an evocative wintry gray palette that paints a bleak, frozen landscape.

The dialogue is sharp and clever. The story relies on slow-burn pacing, plot twists, and an eerie, brooding atmosphere. In fact, everything about *The Pale Blue Eye* is intentionally ominous and dark—everything except Poe. That's precisely what makes the story work: Melling gives us a rendering of Poe that goes against everything we think we know about him.

Compared to Bale's Landor, Melling's Poe is good-natured, compassionate, and sporadically enthusiastic even though he has been singled out for mistreatment by fellow cadets since his arrival. He finds a kindred spirit in Landor, and the two develop a genuine chemistry that highlights each character's strengths and weaknesses. Melling fills Poe with an innate sense of curiosity, immeasurable empathy, and unexpected innocence.

After enjoying the slow-burn murder mystery, the gloomy aesthetic, and the gothic trappings, viewers may find that Cooper jumps the shark with an over-the-top climax that harkens back to shameless b-movie horror finales so common throughout the 1960s. A further dramatic reveal adds another layer to the story, but still fails to live up to the promise of the film's set-up. It's an unsatisfying resolution to such an otherwise well-crafted story.

Though the third act flounders, *The Pale Blue Eye* remains intoxicatingly engrossing. Led by Melling, there are strong performances throughout, including a giallo-level turn by Gillian Anderson as Julia Marquis, and the always reliable Robert Duvall as Jean-Pepe, an occult scholar. Seek it out for its meandering mystery, gorgeous cinematography, and striking dialogue. Most of all, watch it to savor Melling's wonderful portrayal of Poe.

Lee Clark Zumpe is entertainment editor at Tampa Bay Newspapers and an author of short fiction appearing in select anthologies and magazines. Follow Lee at www.patreon.com/Haunter_of_the_Bijou.

The Oubliette by Lee Clark Zumpe

White bones suspended in
descending coils:
perpetual agonies
pooled in stagnant shadow
hovering
above petrified death throes

From the oubliette
only an occasional complaint:
sporadic whimpers tinted gray
with age,
and shallow disembodied whispers

IT CAME FROM INSIDE THE INKWELL!   By Vincent Davis

Do You See What I See?
by
Allan Heller

Rex Bender let out a shriek and dug his fingernails into the armrests of his recliner. The creature in front of him was about three and a half feet tall, with a long nose and a scruffy beard. He was clutching a shillelagh, with which Rex assumed he was proficient. His entire body was dark red. Rex stared wide-eyed at the diminutive demon, who responded with a guttural growl.

Fifteen years into Parkinson's Disease had prepared him for the possibility of occasional hallucinations. But nothing had prepared him for this. At first, they had been flickering, black-and-white images dancing in the periphery of his vision. And they were silent. Now, they were assuming color and clarity, as well as sound. The gnome cocked his head to one side as if studying Rex. Then he floated backward into the darkness, shrinking until he disappeared. Rex remained paralyzed a full five minutes after the apparition vanished. Then fear devolved into self-rebuke. Why had he bothered talking to a figment of his imagination? And why did he shriek when he saw the thing? That was just emasculating.

At breakfast, his wife sensed something was amiss but knew her husband too well to assume that he would broach the subject. So her strategy was a little gentle prodding.

"Did you sleep okay, honey?" she asked.

"Not really," Rex replied sullenly.

She casually mentioned that he hadn't come to bed until late last night.

Rex responded with an edge to his voice. "Who cares what time I go to bed, Donna? I'm retired."

Donna regarded him with a wounded look.

Rex lowered his eyes.

"I'm sorry, honey. I drifted off when I was watching TV, and I had a bad dream. That's all."

That settled it. For now. Christmas season was upon them, and everybody was obligated to "be of good cheer." No nightmares. No monsters. No gnomes. Then he thought, *should've been an elf instead.* He couldn't resist laughing at his own wit.

The following Tuesday, three days later, something happened again.

In the dead of night, Rex and Donna slept in separate beds, necessitated by Rex's occasional thrashing, due to the meds he took to mitigate his Parkinson's. His bed was also fitted with rails on either side. Sometimes, he joked that they may as well strap him down.

He was awake now, listening to his wife's steady, gentle breathing. Everything was good. Everything was fine.

Until it wasn't.

A vaguely human shape was at the bathroom door, about a dozen feet from Rex's bed. Its fuzzy edges sharpened to a discernible silhouette, aided by the faint illumination supplied by the nightlight. It shambled toward him, its progress like that of a drunken vagrant. Rex struggled to a sitting position.

Then everything flashed into focus. The intruder's face was ashen, his eyes bulging.

His head was bent at a 45-degree angle, so that his right ear nearly touched his shoulder. What appeared to be an undershirt or a tube sock was twisted around his neck.

Understanding dawned, and Rex recalled a local middle school teacher, accused of indecent assault of a female student, had hanged himself while awaiting trial. It was all over the news. And now it was in his bedroom.

The apparition addressed him. "Water," it croaked. "I didn't hurt her. Please give me water."

Rex never averted his gaze. He stretched his arm, which began shaking, toward a small nightstand, opened the drawer, and pulled out a .357 Magnum. Rex aimed the prodigious pistol.

"Water."

Rex gritted his teeth. "Damned pervert." And pulled the trigger.

****

Rex grew tired of telling his story to the sergeant. There was an intruder in their bedroom. Rex was in his right to fire his weapon. Of course, there were some details that Rex had thought it better to omit. Like the intruder was the ghost of a suspected pedophile. The official story was that an unknown Caucasian male had somehow made his way into the home of Rex and Donna Bender. Rex didn't get a good look at his face.

Sergeant Linda Meyers wasn't satisfied. How did the burglar, or whatever it was, get into the house? There were no signs of forced entrance. No body. No blood. Only a large hole where the .357 slug had hit the wall.

"Is it possible that you were dreaming or imagining things?" Meyers pressed. She was a tall, slender, 40-something woman with a pretty face and strong feminine curves. Her partner was a strapping patrolman of about 25, whose shirt sleeves struggled to contain his biceps. He had a buzz cut and a dimpled chin. His name tag read "S. Dawson."

"I thought you got rid of that gun years ago, Rex," Donna chided. "Next time, you might kill somebody."

"Got rid of, Donna?" Rex replied. "It's a gun. You don't just toss it into the trash can."

"You've got Parkinson's, for God's sake!" Donna shouted.

Meyers suggested that the police keep the gun until the situation was resolved. Reluctantly, Rex agreed.

"Most likely, DA McKendrick won't file charges," said Meyers. "But I can't speak for her."

With the police gone, Rex and Donna stood alone in their bedroom, trying to make sense of it all. Rex apologized for the commotion, admitting that the "intruder" was likely a hallucination.

"I mean, what else could it have been?" he reasoned. And if it had been an actual ghost, what the hell good would shooting it have done? He agreed to make an appointment with his neurologist, Dr. Emily Barbash, as soon as possible. In the meantime, he just had to hope that he wouldn't be charged with reckless endangerment or risking a catastrophe.

****

Rarely did the face of Dr. Emily Barbash betray any emotion, no matter how joyous or catastrophic the situation. Donna, who had only met the doctor twice, found her to be "quite nice." Rex found her as personable as a stick. But if she could fix this latest crisis, he would never think an unkind thought about her again. Well...

She didn't know how to delicately open a conversation.

"Rex, I understand that you've been seeing things."

Rex shifted in his seat, then rolled his head counterclockwise. This was a side effect of his Parkinson's meds that he had come to accept.

"Everybody sees things," he replied. "I see things that aren't there."

"I understand," she said, unable to sound more patronizing if she tried. "I am going to try to help you, Rex."

Rex had never liked the social protocol which dictated that doctors call patients by first name, whereas patients were supposed to address doctors by title. At 69, he was almost twice the age of his neurologist.

"I see some anomalies with your case, Rex," Dr. Barbash said.

Rex didn't bother to ask her what "anomalies" were.

"These hallucinations come with color and sound. That is atypical. Also, you don't display any obvious signs of psychosis or dementia," she said.

"Maybe I'm seeing ghosts," Rex suggested.

Dr. Barbash laughed politely. She then recommended a drug, Nuplazid®. She briefed Rex on the possible side effects, and advised him to be patient, explaining that the medication typically took several weeks to demonstrate its full potential.

"Is that 'potential' the reduction of symptoms or the side effects?" Rex joked.

The doctor laughed. "Have a good day, Rex."

****

Rex hadn't driven a car in four years. He didn't feel any less of a man as a result. Driving with Parkinson's had been manageable for a decade or so, but eventually Rex had decided to surrender the wheel to his wife. Donna was a careful driver.

Donna pulled into the parking lot of Ziegman's Pharmacy and parked the 2012 Ford Escort.

"Do you want to come in, Rex?"

"No, I'll just hold down the fort," he replied.

She was surprisingly quick. During the ride home, Rex glanced up at the rearview mirror and noticed that Elvis was in the back seat. The King remained silent, and Rex wondered why Elvis wore a seat belt. Rex saw no need to tell Donna about the late crooner, and by the time the Benders were home, the visitor was gone.

Rex had an awful foreboding that night, but nothing happened. He swallowed his first dosage of Nuplazid®, 34 milligrams, at 6:00p.m. as he and Donna finished supper. Steadying himself with the chair and his cane, Rex stood up and announced, "Donna, I feel like a million bucks! I think I'm cured."

Donna laughed. "It should only be, dear. It should only be."

Carefully, Rex pointed his cane at something in the distance.

"It is, my dear. If you don't believe me, go ask that gorilla."

Donna went pale. "Rex, are you — are you...?"

Now Rex laughed. "Just kidding, honey! Just kidding."

Donna scowled. "Rex Alistair Bender, you are not funny!" She stormed out of the kitchen.

"Donna," her husband called after her.

Tuesday, December 20. Rex and Donna were in bed. Rex could discern carolers singing "Silent Night" when he had to use the loo. Rex lowered his left arm rail, got both feet planted on the floor, then heaved himself to a stand with the help of his trusty cane. Glad that he hadn't awakened Donna, Rex shuffled toward his destination.

Rex stood straight, his cane resting against the wall, his left hand clutching the bar, and his right hand helping to aim. He looked into the bathroom mirror, and there he was: the red gnome.

"Hello, Rexie," the fiend said with cheerful sarcasm.

This time, Rex decided to play along.

"Have you ever heard of knocking?"

The gnome unleashed a prolonged, strident cackling, to which Rex responded by turning toward the "red menace" and opening fire. Enraged, the gnome furiously shook his hands and fingers, then brushed the lingering urine from his face and chest.

"I'll kill you!" the gnome shrieked. "I'll kill you for that!"

Rex was defiant. "You won't do shit," he replied. "You're not even real, shorty." Not knowing why, Rex closed his eyes.

The gnome's shouting faded into silence almost instantly. "Don't close your eyes at me! Don't close..."

The pounding of Rex's heart was audible, but he wasn't afraid. A minute passed before he decided to take another glimpse. There was no one there, just a small yellow puddle on the floor. So the little cretin was able to assume solid form, if but briefly. But if his intended victims closed their eyes, the bogey was banished ... at least temporarily. Rex heard his wife calling him desperately. It was time to tell her everything.

****

Antoine Strudel could have hardly had a worse name than he already did. But he little concerned himself with such trivialities. He was neither a comedian nor a baker. The modest home reeked faintly of pungent incense, and candles were lined in rows along the edges of the furniture. Plastic fringes covered the two doorways leading to the kitchen and the dining room. Strudel was seated at a small poker table. Also present and eager to begin were Rex and Donna Bender, who had finally sought from a psychic what doctors and law enforcement officers could not provide.

Strudel explained to the Benders that a plastic table covered with a pentagram and a pentagram rug surrounded the poker table for their protection. The first order of business was to summon the troublesome trio and then trap them.

"Trap them?' Rex asked. "Why don't you just kill them?"

"Because they are already dead, Mr. Bender."

At that point, Strudel excused himself and headed into an adjacent room. Within five minutes, he returned, carrying a thick, leather-bound book, a decanter filled with clear liquid, three porcelain cups, a long wax candle fixed into a silver holder, and a tiny wooden box fitted with a gold lock and key. Seating himself once more, Strudel lit the candle with a long wooden match, filled the porcelain vessels with the contents from the decanter, and instructed the Benders to raise the drinking cups aloft. He began chanting in Latin.

"*Custodi nos, Omnipotens, ab iis terribilibus creaturis quae nobis nocere quaerunt. Hoc elixir eos impotentem reddat."*

At that point, Strudel instructed them to drink, and he did likewise.

"Mr. and Mrs. Bender, you may find this hard to believe, but I have seen many cases over the past 40 years where the victim is a portal for unwelcome visitors," Strudel began. "From what you have told me and what I can discern, this is the case with you." He nodded at Rex.

"Does this mean that I don't really have Parkinson's?" Rex asked.

"On the contrary," Strudel replied. "The Dark Forces have singled you out because you have Parkinson's, Mr. Bender. You make, how shall I say? The perfect portal."

Strudel explained that if one of these beings escaped, they would likely seek Rex's destruction. Every time the spirits manifested, they grew stronger until they became fully enfleshed and more dangerous than anyone could imagine.

"They will then become residents of --to borrow a term from the role-playing game *Dungeons & Dragons*®--the Prime Material Plane. To them, this is much preferable to being tossed down into Hell."

"I wanted to tell you, Mr. Strumpet--"

"Strudel."

"Strudel, right," Rex said. "That time Little Red cornered me in the restroom, I shut my eyes and he disappeared. Didn't come back either."

Strudel nodded. "He may have been low on energy on that particular occasion. But we must strike now. We must kill the ant with a sledgehammer."

Finding another passage in the voluminous Latin tome, Strudel read once more.

"Loquor ad tres inimicos qui noceant Rex Bender. Impero tibi ut appareat. Sed eris, ad tempus, sine vi."

What sounded like a thunderclap exploded in the house, at which point every light extinguished. Strudel fumbled with the large candle on the table, pairing it up with the matches and producing a sufficient flame.

And there they were, hovering two feet above the table. They began glowing with an ethereal light of their own. Donna was mesmerized. Rex wore a smirk of twisted satisfaction as if he were vindicated. Strudel kept a poker face.

The red gnome, floating between "Elvis" and the hanged molester, managed nothing more than a hiss. The others spoke their peace.

"Thank you, thank you very much."

"I would never hurt a child. Do you have water?"

The gnome experienced a brief flash of articulation.

"Piss on me, Bender? I'll piss on you!"

Strudel seized the wooden box and key as he began yet another incantation, this time in English.

"Too long you've avoided a fiery fate. Now inside this box you instead shall wait."

Holding the open box aloft, Strudel watched as Elvis, the gnome, and the pedophile were sucked inside the little wooden sepulcher. He then snapped the lid shut and twisted and removed the key. Rex and Donna were relieved -and terrified.

"You-you sent them to Hell," Rex stammered.

Strudel laughed, brushed some imaginary dust off his shirt, then set the box on the table.

"Not exactly," Strudel replied. "But they will never bother you again, barring any escape from the box."

"They might escape," Donna whispered.

"Why the hell don't you get rid of them?" Rex demanded.

Strudel stood up straight, seeming to get much taller. He picked up the box and held it tightly in his clenched fist. He glowered at Rex.

"Because I am a collector and, thanks to you, I've acquired three new additions." He waved his arm dismissively. "Now leave."

"What about payment?" Rex said.

At once, Strudel seemed calmer and less menacing.

"You don't owe me anything," he said. "This is the best haul I've gotten in over a century." He smiled. "Merry Christmas."

The End

The Story Teller by Matthew Wilson

I wish Daddy didn't tell me stories
When the moonlight hits my door
Now his goodnight kiss is cold
And his breath smells strong of dirt.

Mommy said Daddy would never return
After the hangman did his work
But still, he comes to tell me stories
Like he did when his flesh had blood.

Sometimes his fairy tales have happy endings
But his hugs still give me chills
Though he always leaves before morning
Tapping gently on my door at night.

Mommy would be mad if she knew he was back
She would tell the priest to stake his heart
So I wish Daddy would not tell me stories
For his own good he should stay in his grave.

Monsters & Friends.com by Marc Shapiro

I

I didn't kill him. But I wish I had.

II

They had always sensed that Fred was a monster. Now he had given them proof.

III

They laughed when he said he would live forever.
One hundred years later, he was the one who was laughing.

Gerald's Rose
by
Hillary Lyon

The dusty linen sheet covering her gaunt, supine form rose imperceptibly with each shallow breath. Almost imperceptibly, her eyelids fluttered once under spidery lashes; her full lips twitched in imitation of a quick kiss. Her heartbeats sounded much like water dripping down the sharp point of a stalactite into a shadowy, chilled pool. The sun rose and set outside the rippled glass of her bedroom window. The moon rose and set through its various phases, casting its cold light across the polished tile of her bedroom floor. Thus it was for centuries on end.

In the tiny village which sat in the shadow of this ancient chateau, the townspeople went about their daily lives, generation after generation, working the fields, manning the shops, dancing, courting, and marrying. And in each generation, one young man would look up at the mysterious, derelict chateau, visible just above the tops of the forest trees, and say to himself: *I shall venture forth and take the castle. I shall slay the monster dwelling therein, and I shall free the rumored beauty imprisoned. My people will sing songs of my bravery forevermore.*

So it was in the latest generation that an aspiring adventurer, Gerald by name, took his grandfather's battered sword from its roost over the family's rough stone hearth. He instructed the local blacksmith to sharpen the sword into a deadly edge, to polish it to a fierce luster.

Lastly, Gerald beseeched the parish priest to bless this weapon. As the old priest sprinkled holy water on the blade and mouthed the words the young man longed to hear, he thought to himself: *You sweet, sad fool. I'll be saying a Mass in your memory this time next year.*

Satisfied he was protected by God and armed with a battle-proven blade, Gerald kissed his mother goodbye, hugged Mary, his childhood sweetheart, and set off on the narrow path through the towering forest on the edge of his village.

****

The closer Gerald came to the chateau, the denser the woods grew. The canopy overhead tightened, allowing little sunlight to shine through; in this shadow-thick forest, the black branches blocked his way, and the claw-like twig-ends scratched his face, caught and pulled at his hair and his workman's clothes, as if attempting to hold him back. Determined not to be hindered, he raised his sword in his ungloved hand and slashed his way onward. The branches coughed and shivered as they fell.

At last, Gerald came upon the small, silent clearing encircling the chateau; no birdsong, no cricket chitter, no toad croak, not even a breath of wind disturbed the area. He willed himself to ignore the chill which crept its bony fingertips across his scalp, before tracing a path down his spine. Taking a deep breath to fortify his resolve, Gerald trudged across this dead space to the massive gated entryway set into the mitered stone wall of the chateau. Possessing no sheath, he slid his sword between his wide leather belt and his roughly woven tunic.

Gerald grabbed the weathered iron bars of the gate and shook it. He assumed it would be locked or rusted shut, but to his astonishment, the gate slowly swung open with a painful, creaking wail.

Gerald took one long look at the forest behind him; he questioned whether to go inside or go home. Perhaps he could invent a story about what—or who—he'd found inside, slayed, or rescued. He imagined telling Mary, with her smiling eyes and trusting nature, a tale about his bold adventure—true or not, she'd believe him. Gerald sighed; he knew he couldn't lie to Mary. So with more courage than he felt, he raised his chin, withdrew his sword, and strode inside the chateau's grounds.

The chateau's inner courtyard was as dead as the clearing outside, save for the soft distant ticking of—what? A grandfather clock hidden somewhere deep within one of the chateau's many gilded rooms? No, the ticks were too slow and far between to be from a clock of any kind. Perhaps it was water dripping from some crusted faucet or dying fountain. Maybe it was a slow drip from the ceiling of a secret grotto, one painted with crude renderings of frolicking nymphs and lusty satyrs and—why did his mind wander there? He shook his head to clear his thoughts, scattering the details of these imaginings into nothingness.

The inner courtyard was ringed with stone arches, all filled with brambles. Who would plant such barriers in these doorways? Obviously, someone who didn't want interlopers. Gerald walked to the closest arch and plucked a blackberry from the thorny tangle of vines blocking the way. It was sweetly tart and its sticky dark juice ran down his fingers. He licked it off.

He inspected the next arch, and the next. All were the same, until he came to the fourth arch, which was filled with prickly, snarled rose brambles. *Here*, he said to himself, *here my destiny awaits*. He plucked a single, pink flower from the briar; the wee blossom's inebriating scent filled his head with drowsy peace and overwhelming contentment. Why traipse further into the chateau's interior? Why not take this flower back home to Mary? Sweet, sweet Mary waiting patiently by her cottage door, praying for his return. He slipped the flower into his belt, and once again, shook his head to clear his thoughts.

He lifted his sword, and with brutal stroke after brutal stroke, cleared his way through the arch, only to find a worn stone staircase before him, also barricaded by brambles. His arms ached, but he persisted. Surely there must be a treasure of great worth at the top of the stairs! Or a villainous beast in need of slaughter. Or a legendary beauty in need of—without thinking, he took the rose from his belt and inhaled deeply. He closed his eyes and dreamed. The beauty awaited him upstairs, sleeping, though stirring restlessly under dusty sheets, anticipating her rescue.

He woke, abruptly, and like a man possessed, slashed with frenzy at the choking, thorny growth before him. He ignored the scratches and cuts to his hands and face—the result of the brambles' thorny resistance. His blood made tear-like streaks on his bare skin, thick and dark red like the sticky-sweet nectar of a blackberry.

At the top of the stairs, after the last impeding tangle had been chopped away, Gerald was rewarded for his effort. He came upon a simple wooden door—a door not only unlocked, but slightly ajar. With his heart drumming from effort and excitement, he took a deep breath and pushed inside.

And there she waited, just as he had imagined in his waking dream. He sheathed his sword and approached the ornately carved four-poster bed with the beauty laid out beneath moth-eaten, age-stained sheets. Hesitantly, Gerald touched her cheek—she was as cold as snow-melt. Was he too late? Was she dead?

Panicked, he leaned over her, searching for signs of life. Gerald wasn't sure he heard a faint intake of breath — but he did hear a weak *tick-tick* with long seconds counted between each percussion. A familiar sound, like water dripping from a mineral-encrusted faucet, or a slow drip from the ceiling of a clandestine grotto onto the rough stone floor below. He moved yet closer to her face, examining her perfect features — smooth as a classical marble statue and cut just as sharply. He thought he saw her eyelashes flutter, like the alert, feathered antennae of an exotic insect.

As he looked, a single drop of blood, from a deep bramble-cut on his cheek, rolled down his chin and fell onto the sleeper's cupid's bow of a mouth. The crimson drop disappeared between her lips.

To Gerald's joyous surprise, she licked her lips and opened her eyes — eyes so expansively black he saw comets and stars whirling within them. Gazing into the immense depth of her eyes made him dizzy, made him weak. Before he could say a word, before he could pull away, the beauty grabbed him — with astonishing strength for one who had been bedridden for untold years — and pulled his lanky, writhing body to hers. Alas, his resistance weakened from bramble-hacking, and as she smelled of cloying, bewitching roses...

With a hiss of delight, she opened wide her mouth, and with teeth like the polished tines of a sterling silver carving fork, thrust them deep into the succulent meat of Gerald's neck.

****

There was no heroic struggle, no sudden burst of righteous strength located deep within Gerald's soul. There was only a weary, flailing surrender, accompanied by a cry like the hissing exhalation of a dying beast. Then the stars flashed and swirled and spun away to the deteriorating edge of his awareness, leaving Gerald's eyes empty, and his body a wheezing husk — save for a great all-consuming thirst rooted in the very center of his being.

****

From the doorway of her modest cottage, Mary looked to the chateau, the topmost tower of which was visible above the trees. She spied a light burning in a single window. Was that a sign from Gerald? Had he, indeed, defeated a monster, saved a beauty, found a treasure? Was it possible that he, among all the young men over all the long decades, had attained glory?

Her heart beat in excitement, sending out gong-like ripples into the emerging evening that only Gerald could hear. From the crumbling chateau, the pulsing beat led him home, like a glistening trail of sonic crumbs. This time, the black branches of the forest parted obsequiously before him; the cruel twigs leapt away from his ghostly pale frame. Drained though he was, he did not stumble.

Mary saw him emerge from the gloomy woods; she ran to him with open arms. In the burgeoning twilight, she couldn't see how his eyes had darkened. In her distracted glee, she didn't notice how shallow his breathing had become, how his teeth glittered.

"What did you find?" Mary gasped, hardly able to contain her happiness. Her heart fluttered like a wild bird in a cage of bone.

"A rose," Gerald whispered hoarsely, his floral breath icy against her flushed cheek. "Come see." Taking her warm hand in his chilled one, he led her back down the narrow path into the darkening forest.

The End

A Coward's Second Chance by Matthew Wilson

It is a coward who lives the longest life
And yet he would trade it on a dime
To return to that fated moment long before
When he could have ended a tyrant's line.
Nothing sees so few days as a hero
Those Hercules on the front line die first
So I once withdrew to the sun's safety
Where I was safe from the monster's thirst.
But never-ending nights will always haunt me
Filled with dead faces laughing at my shame
Now the thing with wings has kept his head
And I have failed the holy hunter's game.
My father was a killer of night creatures
Whose roar would chill a vampire's heart
Until he fell and was torn to pieces
A terror that stopped my journey before its start.
I do not recommend the coward's life
Seeing these awful days that should not be
When a vampire king builds his stinking tower
Gorging blood to celebrate his victory
My father's tools have lost their glow
But they install some power in my hand
This old man looking for a second chance
To sweep the stain of flying corpses from the land.

Dark Hearts of Dead Singers by Matthew Wilson

Joyous Julia is a great musician and diva
Before each concert she wanted a room of flowers
A wardrobe filled with the finest clothes
And a bath of blood to cool down after the show.
Artists are known for their eccentricities
Of course, she had a few preshow superstitions
No mirrors, no garlic, and absolutely no crosses
But she always had private time for male fans.
I claimed compensation for my back pain
Dragging the men she briefly loved to the landfill
Digging shallow graves in the little light
So her fans wouldn't tear her posters from their wall in disgust.
I had to admit I was the first of her fan club

Unable to believe my luck when she offered me a kiss
Her fangs hurt my neck but gave me strength
The time to sign her autograph requests as she sleeps.

There is little I would not do for my favorite singer
But like most talents she is a demanding diva
It boils what remains of my blood when her eyes fall on another
But I'm sure if I am patient, she will kiss me again
If I keep her safe in daylight, I'm sure she will sing her songs just for me.

Wrath of the Olitiau!
Echolocation Calls for Two Preternatural Victims
by
Rajeev Bhargava

High-pitched squeaks, followed by scratching and rustling noises, interrupted the older camper as he lay inside the comfort of his tent, writing his journal. It had just turned midnight, yet he was still dressed in mountain gear. He was also working on a thesis for a proposed book on Transylvanian folklore, *Echolocation Calls.*

Outside, the wind blew harshly, blasting against his tent. During winter, he camped in the high altitudes of the northwestern side of the Carpathian Mountains. His name was Professor Alan Fenriche Woodshaw, and he was in his seventies. Although married, he enjoyed his getaways and delved into his lonely lifestyle, enjoying his own company.

He had travelled a long distance to be here in Southeast Europe as it was his dream ambition. His belongings included a large backpack with clothing, a wash-kit, a mixed range of utensils, a lantern, binoculars, a first-aid box, cans of pasta, noodles, tomato and asparagus soups, and last, a steel bottle container and a mobile phone. He had wanted to bring less, but his wife, Daureen, had insisted he take along his laptop as well, which she had gifted him on their paper wedding anniversary. He would use it to chat with her from time to time.

"Oh, even on these barren mountains., there are disturbances. Now, apart from myself, who or what could possibly be up here?"

He turned up the flame of his lantern. To his amazement, he saw the shadows of two bats.

Seconds later, the familiar tone of the video call sounded on his laptop. "Alan, how are you keeping? Have you eaten and taken your pills?"

"Daureen, listen, you've called me at an odd moment. There's something strange trying to enter my tent."

"Please don't go out unless it's essential!"

Once Alan attached the prosthetics to himself, he stood upright. Taking the lantern with him, he crept to the entrance of his tent and unzipped it. Suddenly, two immense bats flew into his inside his tent. One of them, a female, clamped onto Daureen's image on the screen, sank straight through it, and onto her scalp, its eyes glowing bright gold.

The second bat, a male, perched onto Alan's back. An electric spark followed, after which the laptop blipped and went dead.

Moments later, a cloudy mist formed around the bat on Alan's back, and he morphed into a naked elderly man with talons.

Alan reeled back due to his weight. "Get off my back!"

He wriggled left and right until the figure fell off and rolled across the floor.

The elderly man had a pained expression on his face and cried out.

"What do you want from me? asked Alan.

"Blood ... I need ... nourishment..."

He collapsed onto the floor with a pathetic expression on his face.

Alan ran his fingers through his hair and gasped. "What am I going to do now!?"

He searched his backpack and found a tin of tomato soup. He then took out a can opener to remove the lid.

"Oh, I should have heated it," he said to himself. "No problem. He just needs something inside him."

A thought then flashed in his mind. "What if he is ... a vampire? No, if he were, then he'd wear a cloak and have fangs protruding from his mouth. In any case, they're not real."

Alan then tilted the semi-conscious man's head up and said, "Open wide, please."

That was clever of me, he thought. Now I can see if he really is a vampire.

****

At their home, Daureen was going through a similar dilemma. Only, the bat on her head had morphed into an elderly woman.

"No, this can't be real!" Daureen backed away, bumping into the doorknob, and then fled into the hallway. The elderly woman's eyeballs turned a deep red, and her pupils a serpentine yellow. She hissed.

A short time later, Daureen returned, holding a tray of broth and a freshly baked loaf of white bread.

"Oh! Where did she go?"

****

At his tent, Alan had managed to feed a small amount of tomato soup to the ailing vampire, who was now sitting upright but still unable to stand.

"Not as good as the real thing ... but thanks."

Alan raised his eyebrows, trying to figure out what he meant. "Oh! You mean blood. Hah. I didn't know vampires had a sense of humour; that is assuming *you really are a vampire.* I noticed the fangs."

"I became one precisely seventy-seven centuries ago."

Alan didn't believe a word of it, but he felt he could use this encounter with a "vampire" in his thesis, so he went along with his story.

"How interesting. What's your ... aahhhhh!"

The vampire bit into Alan's neck.

"Forgive me, I couldn't resist myself. Now, in a short while, I will gain my youth and the strength to take flight."

"But I don't understand. I just saved your life!" Alan hurriedly bandaged his wound.

"Save the undead? What balderdash!" The vampire, still naked, burst into a fit of laughter.

"Hah, hah, hah, hah, hah, hah, hah, hah, hah!" He raised his arms upwards, morphed into a wolf, and ran out of the tent, howling triumphantly.

****

By the time Daureen returned to the kitchen, the elderly lady was gone.

"Now I am scared. I wonder where she could be?" She turned left and right, then began searching. Just then, from the ceiling above her head, the vampire bat fell onto her, clamping itself to her face and taking a bite from her jugular.

"Aaaahhhhrrrrgggeeuugee!" Daureen collapsed.

The bat changed back into a much younger and attractive woman with long talons on her fingers and toes. She gazed at Daureen menacingly, hissed, and left hurriedly.

****

As Alan made his way out of the tent, the winds almost pushed him off the cliff. He walked cautiously ahead until he saw a narrow crack in the mountain. When he reached it, he pointed his lantern toward it.

"A crevice, how odd. I'm certain that was not there before."

Alan crept inside and found himself inside a large, illuminated cave.

"Back already!" called a female voice.

Alan felt his pulse race. He turned to leave when a beautiful woman appeared.

"I'm sorry to intrude. I had no idea that people live in these hostile mountains."

"Yes. I live with my children in this cave. It has been our home for many centuries.

"One of them, my son, is what you humans call a Muroni, often mistaken for a vampire. He's the more friendly of the two. Very boisterous; he loves to play around."

"And what about the other one?"

She walked up to him, circling like a huntress stalking her prey, then smirked.

"The 'other one,' as you crudely put it, is my daughter. She's referred to as a Vorcalac. Often mistaken for a werewolf, ever so quiet. Always keeps herself to herself. Doesn't trust people, especially humans … like your wife. Oh, did I mention she loves her shape-shifting? Hah, hah!"

"I'm sorry, but I don't believe a word of it."

"No, I didn't think you would." She eyed him up and down. "You're a brave man, venturing here all on your own."

"You didn't ask me who I am," said Alan.

"Does it matter?"

"Maybe." You know, you're amazing. We think you're incredible. Yet you play the fool."

"Now, you're talking in riddles. Wait a minute," said Alan. "If what you say *is* true, then…"

"Let me clue you in. Does the word *shapeshifter* ring any bells, Fenriche'?"

Just then, a black mist formed around her. Alan sensed danger and turned to run to the crevice entrance. As he tried to slide through the gap, it slid inwards, narrowing enough to trap him.

He struggled with all his force.

The mist cleared to reveal an elusive, immense black-bodied bat with a wingspan of 12 feet. It gazed menacingly at its helpless victim and opened its mouth to reveal its serrated teeth with long fangs. Its mouth oozed with mucus from its shrivelled lips. And then, the same loud squeak echoed across the cave.

It flapped its mighty wings and caught Alan around his shoulders with its sharp talons and said, face to face with him: "The last piece of knowledge you shall ever acquire in this lifetime is that *I* am known as the Olitiau, and you are about to face my wrath. Goodbye!"

In one bite, it decapitated Alan with its fangs.

"Come on in, children! I've caught a fresh kill for you."

The Muroni son came running in on all fours and greeted his mother.

"Where's your sister?"

He smiled wickedly. "Oh, she decided to eat out." And they tucked in.

Elsewhere, perched on the privacy of a tree branch, the Vorcalac, in her bat form, had just finished devouring the remains of Daureen's brain, then gave out a loud triumphant hiss. She took flight to return home to her mother.

The End

Lantern in the Snow
by
Marge Simon

This is a night that won't leave me alone. I can't sleep, so I grab my parka for a walk along the water. Ice spiders come with the fog and spin rainbows in the chilly air.

Someone is playing a jazz harp; forms move in the flickering light. I stop to watch, but they turn to shadows.

I come to a lantern fully lit on a wall covered in snow. Gazing into it, I see a woman's form. So strange, a thing like this. I touch it, my fingertips chase her reflection in the glow of the cold glass. She drifts there, this ghostly doll, beyond my reach, her face lit with something beyond words, familiar and not. Her image reminds me of a former lover, Iris. A hellion in bed, she was. Quite inventive too, crazy about me—but I was young. I said goodbye, she screamed a curse—and that was that. A stream of others took my fancy. Mesmerized, I watch as the flame within the box flickers out.

The sea bucks in a mad frenzy. A passionate goddess, copulating with the rising wind.

Now I can smell Iris' perfume, feel her breath upon my neck. I run forward to meet her as she bids, into the icy waves.

The End

Nasty Planetary Alignment
by
Christopher T. Dabrowski

I do not know too much about astrology, horoscopes, and planetary alignments. And explaining another military conflict with some war planet entering something sounded like total nonsense to me.

When the Earth was taken over by Artificial Intelligence, I thought this nonsense would finally stop—because who would be at war with whom now?

A week before the First World Robot War, Alison declared that planetary alignments indicated a major global conflict loomed at any moment.

Again, obviously, I didn't believe it.

And I could have taken the credit and driven with her to an exotic island...

The End

Love Forever Blood Forever by Marc Shapiro

It's night
When the moon is motionless in blood red relief
It's the perfect backdrop
For the lovers who have come out to play
Their foreplay had been to feed
Now the demons will love
They fondle, entwine
Their passion in full bloom
After their night of bloody business
They have been doing it this way
Seemingly forever
Decades
Eons
Forevers
Blood then lust
Once it started the routine was inevitable
it could not be stopped
The blood lust and the passion would never go away
Because the only alternative in their lives
Was death
Among the living

Is Jack Back? by Marge Simon

A prayer card in the hands of a victim,
a young woman who worked in a brothel,
one of a thousand in Whitechapel, 1890.

Hers was a clean wound made by skilled hands,
yet the organs were untouched, nothing ghastly,
merely a puncture in her neck to drain her blood –
by transfusion, giving hope to a dying child?

But that, of course, would make no sense,
for death would be a blessing for street urchins,
and The Ripper's *modus operandi* didn't fit,
he'd have no concern for dying children.

Scotland Yard was baffled by this mystery;
then came a message from a Madam Balfour:
"When his victims saw him,
They fell down before him"

The consensus was he'd put the woman in a thrall,
and took her by the jugular as the Undead do,
thus, he had to be related to the Count,
with no ties at all to Master Jack.

I Envy Him So Much That It Makes Me Squirm
by
Christopher T. Dabrowski

That turd has everything I've always wanted, and it came to him with no effort. And that's because where I made poor choices, he made good ones.

This got him the perfect woman and wealth.

Moreover, he hasn't lived through all these massacres. I don't think he even knows what suffering is. Yes, I am richer with different experiences, but so what? I didn't ask for such attractions.

Yes, I've met myself from an alternate reality, and I envy him so much that I hate him—and it's just me after all....

How about killing him and taking his place?

The End

Line Forms to the Night by Marc Shapiro

Follow me
Into the blackness
Into Hell
Because I am the night
I know what tempts you
What drives you with desire
To have it all
I know what it was like
To take that final step
To the other side
I can assure you
That it will only hurt for a minute
Before you enter eternity
And you will be home free
Forever

About the Contributors

Linda Barrett:

    Ms. Barrett has been writing all her life. She wrote her first book at the age of eight. It's still in the McKinley Elementary school library. She was published in the *Huntingdon Junior Library* literary magazine by age thirteen. She's won three awards with the Montgomery County Community College Writer's contest. "Mr. Cat's Revenge" won third place in the 2014 MCCC contest. Ms. Barrett lives with her 84 years young mother in Abington in the same house for 50 years."

Rajeev Bhargava:

    Rajeev Bhargava has been writing since birth and is now a creative multi-genre writer and artist. His career includes public articles, illustrations, poems, and stories published in dark fantasy and horror, science fiction and fantasy, an assorted poems and haiku collection of love and romance, comedy, wit, and humor and the welfare of animals, plants and concern for our green environment. Just recently, he completed a children's storybook for Christmas, Easter, and Halloween, all under the pen name Silver Phoenix. Rajeev's first work, a dark fantasy chiller, appeared in 1990 for *Peeping Tom* titled "Old Crow." Rajeev is thankful to Jesus for his talent; he's working on a new book this Halloween titled *Terrifying and Bloodcurdling Scary Stories for Sshh!!! ...It's Halloween.* Rajeev is single and lives with his parents and five pet Chihuahuas. He's writing a romantic novel entitled *Love Will Find a Way.* He's attained an Arts and Humanities BA (HONS) in Literature and an English Literature Teaching Certificate. When he's not writing, he enjoys video, photography, acting, fashion, modeling, ceramics, and pottery.

Christopher T. Dabrowski:

    Christopher has had numerous books published in the USA and Poland. His USA works include: *Anomaly* and *Escape*, both published by the Royal Hawaiian Press. Books published in Poland include *Anima Vilis* (Initium), *Grobbing* (Novae Res), *Deathbirth and other Stories* (Agharta & Amoryka), *Orgazmokalipsa* (Alternatywne publishing house), *Anomalia* (Forma publishing house), and *Ucieczka* (2017 - Dom Horroru publishing house). Monika Olasek provided the English translation for his *Night to Dawn* stories.

Sandy DeLuca:

    Sandy has written five novels; *Settling in Nazareth* (she painted the cover art), *Descent, Manhattan Grimoire, From Ashes,* and *Requiem for the Dead.* Her poetry chapbook, *Burial Plot in Sagittarius* (also created cover art and illustrations), was nominated for the BRAM STOKER award in 2001. Her art has been exhibited in galleries, hair salons, book stores and online venues. She has also painted covers and contributed interior illustrations for various numerous small press venues.

Kendall Evans:

    Kendall Evans' stories and poems have appeared in nearly all the major science fiction and fantasy magazines, including *Asimov's SF, Analog, Weird Tales, Strange Horizons, Weirdbook, Mythic Delirium, Dreams & Nightmares, Space & Time, Nebula Award Showcase (2012), The Magazine of Speculative Poetry, Amazing Stories, Fantastic Stories, Spectral Realms* and many others. He is the author of the novels *The Rings of Ganymede* and *The Adventures of Ching Shih, Pirate Princess.*

Chris Friend:

    Chris has published his art in small press horror magazines for nearly 25 years. His surreal horror images have been featured in *Stygian Articles, Realm of the Vampire, Deathrealm, Black Petals,* and *Space and Time.* He draws his inspiration from Harry Clarke, H. R. Giger, and the horror comics of the 70s such as the Tomb of Dracula her and the Hammer Studios Frankenstein films. Chris friend can be reached at Mars_art_13@yahoo.com. Chris friend can be reached at Mars_art_13@yahoo.com.

To sample his illustrations, go to http://chris.michaelherring.net and http://www.moonlit-path.com/art-2-13-06.htm.

Todd Hanks:

The creative writing of Todd Hanks has been seen in publications such as Asimov's Science Fiction Magazine and the Kansas City Star newspaper.

Hal Kempka:

Hal's stories have been published in numerous magazines and ezines including *Night to Dawn, Blood Moon Rising, Black Petals, Inner Sins, Sanitarium, Yellow Mama,* and *Microhorror.* His horror short fiction anthologies, *Blue Plate Special* and *Discarded Treasures,* are currently available on Amazon Kindle, Barnes and Noble, and Smashwords, among others. *Discarded Treasures* is available in both paperback and e-book. Other anthologies including his stories are Pill Hill Press: *Zombie Art Inspired Short Stories, Blood Bound Books: Seasons in the Abyss,* and Post Mortem Press: *Shadowplay.*

David C. Kopaska-Merkel:

David C. Kopaska-Merkel, a semi-retired geologist, won the 2006 Rhysling award for best long poem (for a collaboration with Kendall Evans), and edits *Dreams & Nightmares* magazine (since 1986). He has edited *Star*line,* an issue of *Eye To The Telescope,* and several *Rhysling* anthologies, co-edited the 2023 Dwarf Stars anthology, has served as SFPA president, and is an SFPA Grandmaster. His poems have been published in *Asimov's, Analog, Strange Horizons,* and more than 200 other venues. His latest collection, *Some Disassembly Required,* winner of the Elgin award, was published by Diminuendo Press in 2022. Blog: https://dreamsandnightmaresmagazine.blogspot.com/

April Lafleur:

April Lafleur's distinctive painting style is inspired by German Expressionism, emphasizing the artist's deep-rooted feelings or ideas, evoking powerful reactions-abandoning reality, characterized by simplified shapes, bright colors, gestural marks and brush strokes. Masters like Kirshner and Marc come to mind when viewing April's dynamic paintings.

April has earned an AFA at the Community College of Rhode Island, where she had the privilege of studying with Bob Judge, a masterful painter who has worked as an artist for over sixty years. He continues to mentor and inspire her today. In addition, she studied art at Rhode Island College. Today, her paintings are maintained in private collections. She exhibits in New England presently and is working to place her figurative work with print magazines beyond the local area.

Her studio is located at the Agawam Mill in Rhode Island, where she works long hours to perfect her craft. Website: www.aprillafleurart.com.

Hillary Lyon:

With an MA in English Literature from SMU, Hillary Lyon founded and for 20 years served as senior editor for the independent poetry publisher, Subsynchronous Press. Her speculative, horror, and sci-fi stories have appeared in numerous print and online publications. She's also an illustrator for horror/sci-fi, and pulp fiction sites. And she loves to hand-paint furniture and accessories.

Rod Marsden:

Rod Marsden hails from Sydney, Australia. He has three degrees related to writing and history. His stories have been published in Australia, England, Russia, the USA and now Canada. He has work in the American anthology *Cats Do it Better,* the American steam punkanthology *Break Time* and in the Canadian anthology *Morbid Metamorphosis.* Many of his short stories have been published in *Night to Dawn* magazine. His books include *Undead Reb Down Under and Other Vampire Stories, Disco Evil: Dead Man's Stand, Ghost Dance,* and *Desk Job* (his salute to Lewis Carroll). *Cold Water Conscience* is his venture into Crime/Horror. His short play, *Zombie Vision,* was well received at Cronulla Arts Theatre. His play *Hyde and Seek* was even better received. Rod has a fondness for Cronulla and the Wollongong area but an abiding love for the more northern Clarence River region of his home state of New South Wales.

Denny E. Marshall:

Denny E. Marshall has had art, poetry, and fiction published. Some recent credits include interior art in *Midnight Echo #14* Dec. 2019, cover art for *Society Of Misfit Stories* Feb. 2020, and poetry in *Space & Time Magazine #134* Fall 2019. This year his website is celebrating 20 years on the web. Also in 2020 his artwork is for sale for the first time. It is available on Zazzle as posters coffee cups, puzzles, mouse pads, etc. The link is on his website. (Click on top left drawing.) See more at www.dennymarshall.com.

Elizabeth Hattie Pierce-Collins:

Elizabeth first learned art and drawing from her mother. From there, she was self-taught until she was able to attend art school. She loves drawing the human figure and never stops studying the human body in motion. Her illustrations have appeared in *Night to Dawn* magazine and *The Spider's Web* (a novel). These have drawn positive attention from the readers. Elizabeth hopes to appear in more magazines and books in the future. For more information, contact Elizabeth at wackyursalinan45@aol.com.

Marc Shapiro:

Marc Shapiro is within spitting distance of 100 published books. Recent additions include the books *Bukowski: On Film, Pete Brown: The Poet Who Rocks,* and coming next year, *Abracadabra: The Steve Miller Story.* Also lurking in the shadows: *Atomic Rooster.* When Marc Shapiro works, he works hard. By the time you read this, he will have written a hundred more.

Marge Simon:

Marge Simon's works appear in publications such as DailySF Magazine, Pedestal, Dreams& Nightmares. She edits a column for the HWA Newsletter, "Blood & Spades: Poets of the Dark Side," and serves as Chair of the Board of Trustees. She won the Strange Horizons Readers Choice Award, 2010, and the SFPA's Dwarf Stars Award, 2012. She has won three Bram Stoker Awards ® for Superior Work in Poetry, two first place Rhysling Awards and the Grand Master Award from the SF Poetry Association, 2015. In addition to her poetry, she has published two prose collections: *Christina's World,* Sam's Dot Publications, 2008 and *Like Birds in the Rain,* Sam's Dot, 2007. Her poems appear in *Qualia Nous* (Written Backwards), *The Dark Phantastique* (Jasunni Productions), Spectral Realms anthologies by S.T. Joshi, and more poems will appear in *Chiral Mad 3* and *Scary Out There,* a HWA/ Simon & Schuster Y/A collection, 2015. www.margesimon.com

Lonnie D. Weems:

Every school has one: "the kid who can draw." Lonnie spent his youth being that kid. When he wasn't drawing, Lonnie could generally be found in front of the TV repeatedly watching every horror and science fiction movie or show that popped up. His favorites tend toward the Gothic: Universal, Hammer and Mario Bava films. Following a decade of military service and still more years of raising a family, Lonnie has decided to unleash "the kid who can draw" again.

Matthew Wilson:

Matthew Wilson has been published repeatedly in *Star*Line, Night to Dawn Magazine, Hiraeth Publishing,* and many more. His first story collection, *Gargoyles of the Abbey,* is now available on kindle.

Lee Clark Zumpe:

Lee Clark Zumpe has been writing and publishing horror, dark fantasy and speculative fiction since the late 1990s. His short stories and poetry have appeared in a variety of publications such as *Weird Tales, Space and Time* and *Dark Wisdom;* and in anthologies such as *Dark Horizons, Best New Zombie Tales Vol. 3, Dread Shadows in Paradise, Heroes of Red Hook* and *World War Cthulhu.* His work has earned several honorable mentions in *The Year's Best Fantasy and Horror* collections.

An entertainment columnist with Tampa Bay Newspapers, Lee has penned hundreds of film, theater and book reviews and has interviewed novelists as well as music industry icons such as Paddy Moloney of The Chieftains and Alan Parsons. His work for TBN has been recognized repeatedly by the Florida Press Association, including a first-place award for criticism in the 2013 Better Weekly Newspaper Contest.

Lee lives on the west coast of Florida with his wife and daughter. Visit www.leeclarkzumpe.com.